MEMAW'S TURQUOISE NUGGETS

Memaw's
TURQUOISE
NUGGETS

Helping Children of all Ages Manifest Good Fruit

DEBORAH CAMACHO

Book One
in the Turquoise Nuggets Series

XULON ELITE

Xulon Press Elite
2301 Lucien Way #415
Maitland, FL 32751
407.339.4217
www.xulonpress.com

Memaw's Turquoise Nuggets
P.O. Box 123
Vail, AZ 85641
www.memawsturquoisenuggets.com
sharewithmemaw@memawsturquoisenuggets.com

Paperback ISBN-13: 978-1-6628-5077-6
Ebook ISBN-13: 978-1-6628-5078-3

Introduction

Grandmas are known for offering "pearls of wisdom". The term generally means *valuable advice*. This Memaw has wisdom gleaned from the Bible to share with her grandkids to raise another generation of ambassadors for Christ. Coming from the Southwest, she shares her tidbits of advice as "turquoise nuggets" instead. Join us as Memaw shares *Turquoise Nuggets* with her grandchildren...and you!

Dedication

Dedicated with love to
Iliana, Danae, Josiah, Nathanael, Andrina, Levi and Linnea.

TABLE OF CONTENTS

1.

OLIVIA

"Defend the poor and fatherless;
Do justice to the afflicted and needy."
Psalm 82:3

She looked left, then right. Holding her breath Olivia picked up a brick and threw it into the back door's window. Not tall enough to reach in to unlock it, she looked around, and with heart pounding, dragged a porch chair to the door. Stood on it and reached in with a feeling of shame and relief. *By the looks of this house, the people must have money to fix the window. They probably have a lot of food, too.*

"Uhh, blood," she whispered, pulling her arm back and wiping it on her shirt.

She went straight for the refrigerator and guzzled half a carton of milk. She gasped for a breath after the last gulp.

A neighbor's dog barked and growled. Ignoring the bark, she reached in for a foil package in the shape of a triangle. She wasn't halfway done with the pizza when she heard the dog's bark change pitch, then footsteps around the side of the house.

1

Leaving the refrigerator door open and the carton of milk on the floor she ran, wide-eyed and chest heaving, through the living room and down the hall to the first door. A bathroom. The window was too high to climb through.

She tried the next room—a bedroom, but that window led to the back yard. Surely, she'd run into the people who were at the back door by now.

Olivia crossed the hall to a bedroom with a window that led to the front yard. Jumping onto the bed she unlatched it and pushed against the screen. It bent until it gave way and fell to the floor. Her foot caught on the sill as she climbed out but she righted herself, dropped to the ground and ran.

She was free.

She rounded the hedge at the end of the driveway and came face-to-face with a police officer. She even startled him.

Caught. She stopped and fell like a lump on the sidewalk.

I will not cry. They can't take me back. I will not go back, as the tears welled in her eyes at her unsuccessful attempt to escape.

The police officer reached for his handcuffs, shook his head in disbelief as he reached for her hand. "You again? When will you stop running?"

Officer Sam attended Grace Community Church with Memaw and Papa James. During the share-a-dish after church, he'd asked Papa, "If I could arrange it with the court, would you be willing to take in a 12-year-old girl who needs love

2

and a constant watchful eye? She's a flight risk at every foster home she's in."

"I'll certainly talk to Memaw and we'll pray about it," he said. "When do you need to know?"

"Need to know what?" Memaw walked up with a smile, reaching over Papa's shoulder to get a chocolate from the candy bowl.

"Her name's Olivia. She's 12 and she's been in and out of foster homes her entire life. I arrested her for breaking and entering and illegal trespass," explained Sam. "Right now, she's sitting in the Juvenile Detention Center awaiting her court hearing but has no family, no friends, not even a foster parent that would show up for her. It's a sad situation and I'll admit I have a soft spot in my heart for her. If I didn't have three children around her age at home—two of them boys, my wife and I would take her in. I'm asking if you two would consider taking her in?"

"The way I see, we're responsible for the widows and orphans. If no one else is doing it, and we can, and we feel the Holy Spirit's leading toward this, we should obey," said Memaw. "Let's pray about it," she extended her hands.

"Right now?" asked Papa.

"Sure, why not?" she grabbed Papa's hand and offered her other to Sam and invited his wife to join them.

"Father, Your dear child is alone," Papa prayed. "We are called to take care of the widows and orphans for You. If this is something You would have us do, please make it very clear. Lead and guide us to know what she needs and how we are to proceed in her best interest and in Your will we pray, in Jesus' name."

As Papa said, "Amen," Sam's cell phone rang.

He took the call and returned with a grim face. "Olivia's court hearing is Tuesday morning at 9:45."

"Can we be there?" asked Memaw.

"I suppose. But have you even decided yet? You really need to talk about this and consider the commitment it will be. You cannot leave her unattended—ever."

"We've got the room and most importantly, we have love to offer her. What more do we need?" answered Memaw.

"God's consent and leading," said Papa, matter-of-factly.

"I feel we have it. He hasn't said, 'no' so it must be a 'yes and amen'," she smiled.

Papa shook Sam's hand, "We'll be there Tuesday morning. We're not yet saying 'yes', though."

"Good enough."

Tuesday morning Memaw woke earlier than usual to bake a batch of cookies and arrange food in a crock pot for dinner. She and Papa had spent the last two days praying and discussing what it would mean to bring home a 12-year-old girl at their age, and how they could be certain she would always be supervised.

They left the house with time to find parking in busy downtown and walk to the courthouse.

They found Sam sitting behind a desk in the courtroom. They waved at him and sat in the second row.

Court proceedings would begin in nine minutes, if they ran on time. Sam turned and whispered back to them, "Olivia's case is seventh."

Memaw turned to Papa, "We don't even know her last name."
He squeezed her hand.

They were five cases in when a man in uniform walked in
with a young girl. Her curly hair stuck out from two hairbands
that attempted to hold in thick side braids, but not very well.
She wore an old, dirty Vacation Bible School t-shirt stained
with blood and two sizes too big for her. Pants that looked
two sizes too small. She was quiet and withdrawn. She looked
afraid but sat where she was told and didn't move.

When it was Olivia's turn, a lady behind a desk read her
name, Olivia Simpson, and the charges filed against her.

The judge asked, "Miss Simpson, why did you break
into a house?"

Nervously pulling on the bandage that covered her hand
Olivia spoke with her head down, "I was hungry. I wanted
something to eat. I'm sorry I broke their window, but I didn't
take anything...other than the food I ate." She didn't argue to
defend herself.

Officer Sam was called and he gave the details of his
arrest. He asked to approach the bench and the judge waved
him forward.

Memaw glanced at Papa and squeezed his arm she was
clinging to. Papa took a deep breath.

"Your honor, as you know, the defendant is a ward of the
State," Officer Sam said, "I'd like to request that she be released
at this time to two people in the audience today. Their names
are James and Dolores Torres."

"You know them, Officer?"

"I do and can attest to the fact they will be good guardians
of Miss Simpson and offer this young lady a healthy, safe and
loving home life."

"James and Dolores Torres please approach the bench."

Memaw glanced at Olivia as she walked up. She seemed bewildered by the proceedings.

"Do you agree to take on the care of Olivia Simpson?"

"We do, your honor," answered Papa.

After more questions and the shuffling of papers, the judge brought down his gavel. "I now award the legal guardianship and custody of Olivia Simpson to Mr. and Mrs. James Torres."

And that is how Olivia came to live with the Torres family.

On the drive home they attempted to have conversation with Olivia. She wouldn't answer many questions, so Memaw told her about themselves. They asked Olivia to call them "Papa" and "Memaw". They seem nice enough, but she's seen that before. They told her they have seven children and each of them are married and have kids of their own. That's a big family for Olivia to suddenly find herself in. More people to protect herself from.

It was difficult for Memaw to know what Olivia was thinking or feeling. She was quiet and guarded. Olivia was determined not to get too comfortable. Perhaps she figured they would be sending her back to the foster system as soon as she became more work than she was worth—that's how things usually ended for her—if she didn't run away, first.

What Olivia didn't realize was that this time, Memaw and Papa weren't getting paid to foster her.

2.

BORN OF WATER AND SPIRIT

"Most assuredly, I say to you, unless one is born again,
he cannot see the Kingdom of God."
John 3:3

"Good morning, Olivia, did you sleep well?" asked Memaw peeking her head into the room.

Olivia turned her back to the door, "Yeah."

"I'm glad to hear it. Breakfast is ready, how about you get washed up and dressed so we can call Papa in to eat?"

"I don't have clothes," mumbled Olivia.

"I put clothes on the table in the bathroom for you," said Memaw.

Without saying a word, Olivia went to the bathroom. She looked in the mirror and wondered how she wound up here. From the room she heard Memaw ask, "What are your favorite colors?"

"I don't know."

"Well, you think on it and let me know."

No response.

"I was thinking we could make some curtains and pillows in those colors to make your room feel personal to you."

Olivia made a face in the mirror, *Why is she doing all this? I won't even be here long.*

Olivia walked out of the bathroom and Memaw handed her the corners of the quilt. She taught Olivia how to make the bed, tucking the corners in neatly.

"My son, John and his family, are coming to spend the day with us. He's married to Andrea and they have two boys and three girls. It'll be a fun day."

The morning dragged on with one-sided conversations. Even through breakfast with Papa. There was enough work to keep everyone busy, so that helped break up the awkwardness.

Memaw asked Olivia to help feed the animals, directing her to the feed bin for each animal and telling her how much feed to give, all while she milked the goat.

She would never let it be known, but Olivia found it fascinating. She'd never seen an animal milked before. Although nervous to be around the animals, without admitting it, she liked feeling useful and enjoyed the chores on the farm.

The crisp morning air against her face and arms felt refreshing. There was something happening inside she couldn't describe. Her insides were fed with more than just food—she was spoken to with kindness. She was made to feel welcomed here. Of course, she wondered how long it would last. She constantly reminded herself not to get too comfortable, as her stay here wouldn't last. It never did at any home. Why would this time be any different?

As she stood outside the horse's stall waiting for the water trough to fill, she'd reach in to stroke the horse's mane. He bobbed his head.

"His soft nose is nice to touch," said Memaw watching the interaction from the other side of the goat.

For the first time since coming to the farm, Olivia smiled as she touched Geronimo's velvety nose. As if he understood, he didn't bob his head and allowed her to enjoy the experience.

She wondered if the horse was able to be ridden but didn't dare ask. It didn't matter anyway.

After chores, Olivia sat at the kitchen island. Memaw pulled out a glass gallon jar. "Would you please hand me a filter from the box on the middle shelf against the wall?" she asked.

Step-by-step, Memaw talked through what she was doing. She'd occasionally ask Olivia to do, get, or toss something.

What did this lady do when I wasn't here? thought Olivia. *She sure does need a lot of help.*

Memaw didn't really need help getting chores done. Having raised seven children, she knew that putting her children to work alongside her was doing more than getting help with chores. She was teaching them good work ethics, how to serve others, and life skills that set them up to be independent thinkers.

John and his family arrived and introductions were made. Right away the granddaughters asked Olivia to play in the fort. She had seen it from the barn that morning. Olivia looked over to Memaw for unspoken permission.

"Have fun," she said smiling and pouring two glasses of lemonade for her and Andrea to drink on the front porch.

The boys ran off to saddle the horses. John was with Papa in the shop.

Annette left the group of girls to come over and ask to go for a walk. "I've already been for my walk this morning," her mom said.

"Olivia and I would like to go on a walk with you," volunteered Memaw. She called for Olivia but there was no answer. "Olivia."

Memaw looked at Annette, "Where are the girls?"

"Elizabeth and Addy are at the fort. Olivia left."

Memaw walked toward the fort, her heart beating faster. "Olivia, let's go for a walk!" No answer. "Where did she go?"

Annette shrugged.

"Olivia, answer me!"

From the fort they walked to the barn and to the back end of the property. Then they went to the shop to tell Papa Olivia couldn't be found.

"Come on, Elizabeth," Andrea said, "Let's look in the house."

John headed to his truck but Papa held up his hand and told him to wait. He pointed to the large mesquite tree north of the arena.

Memaw found Olivia perched on a branch watching the boys rope horseback in the arena. Out of breath, she said, "Olivia, I need you to answer when we call you, I didn't know where you were."

"I don't want to play in the fort."

"You don't have to, but you do need to let me know where you are."

Olivia didn't answer.

"Please respond so I know you heard and understood me."

"I understand, okay?"

"Thank you. Annette and I are going for a walk, will you please come down and walk with us?"

"I'd rather watch them ride the horses."

"You can watch them when we get back, let's go for a short walk before it gets too hot. Come on down," said Memaw.

With a roll of her eyes, Olivia jumped off the branch and dusted her pants. She walked a few paces behind Memaw and Annette forcing them to walk slower than their normal pace. *They're so dumb they don't even know what direction the letter 'z' goes,* she thought to herself, as if saying something mean would make her feel better. The farm's front entryway had a sign hanging from the top horizontal pole that said, 'Cozy Acres Farm' and the letter 'z' was backwards.

"Tell me again the story of when I was born, Memaw?" asked Annette.

Thinly scattered white clouds painted the sky and Memaw's eyes sparkled. "It was one of the favorite days of my life."

"The house where you live wasn't finished yet. The windows had just been installed so your momma was more and more hopeful the house would be done in time for when you would be born. She really wanted to give birth to you in your own home."

"But I was born in your house, right?"

"That's right. I've always thought since you were born in our house, you should be ours, but your momma and daddy haven't agreed to that. They want to keep you, I guess." Memaw smiled, waiting for the look of delight on Annette's face.

Memaw turned and smiled at Olivia and realized she was more than a few paces behind. "We're gonna have to step it up a beat to get home and fix lunch."

"Tell me the rest," Annette said.

"Well, the evening you decided you were ready to meet your family finally came. Your momma couldn't tell if she was experiencing false labor or if it was the real deal."

"It was the real deal, wasn't it?"

"Indeed, it was. After a short nap, your momma took a bath and was ready for your arrival."

Annette looked up with delight. "Tell me about how I soaked Daddy wet."

"You soaked him, alright. You came shooting out as the bag of water you'd lived in burst. Your daddy caught you like a football and juggled your slippery body."

"But he didn't drop me."

"No, fortunately, he didn't. Instead, we invited Papa and your brothers and sister to meet you. We all rejoiced over your arrival. We cried, and laughed and thanked God you were here and given to us."

"Then Daddy lifted me up like Simba."

"Your daddy lifted you up to our Heavenly Father and said, 'Thank You, Father, for the blessing of this child. We dedicate her life to You, and our lives to raising her in the admonition of Your Word and for Your service.' "

Annette walked in silence, taking in the details again. Olivia walked a little closer, but still remained behind. A cool, gentle breeze blew and Memaw smiled as the reminder that Holy Spirit was ever-present.

"You know, that reminds me of a Bible story," Memaw said, "Do you want to come up with us to listen to a story, Olivia?"

Olivia didn't answer and intentionally walked slower instead.

Memaw went on with her story, "It's about a man named Nicodemus."

"Nic-o-dē-mus," sounded out Annette. "I like that name, it's different."

"Yeah, it is different."

"Tell us about Nicodemus."

"Well, one night, Nicodemus had gone to talk with Jesus and said, '*Surely You are from God, sent to us to teach us. No one can do these signs that You do unless God is with him.*' Jesus answered Nicodemus and said, '*Truly, truly, I say to you, unless one is born again he cannot see the Kingdom of God.*'

Just like you, Nicodemus knew that he'd been born from his momma's womb. But Jesus was talking about being *born again?* He didn't understand. So Nicodemus asked, '*How can a man be born when he is old? He cannot enter a second time into his mother's womb and be born again, can he?*' " [1]

Annette scrunched her face and said, "We couldn't fit."

"No, it's not a physical rebirth Jesus was talking about. He was talking about a spiritual rebirth."

"Oh," was all Annette said. It was clear to Memaw she didn't fully understand.

"Jesus told him, '*Do not be amazed that I said to you, you must be born again. Truly, truly, I say to you, unless one is born of water and the Spirit, he cannot enter the Kingdom of God.*' [2] That we must be born of water and of the Spirit means we have a washing over us by the Spirit of God. That washing from the Spirit is a work from God above, not from man." [3]

They walked along in silence. Before Memaw realized it, Olivia was now walking beside her. It made her smile inside.

"Nicodemus studied the Old Testament. Knowing this, Jesus told him in a way he could understand according to Old Testament teaching. Washing with water meant becoming clean

---

[1] John 3:1-4

[2] John 3:5

[3] John 7:38-39

and pure among the Jews.[4] Getting clean and pure by the Spirit symbolizes the forgiveness of sins." [5]

"Oh, it's like taking a bath to get washed clean!" said Annette.

"Yes! Remember Jesus' words to Nicodemus? '...*unless one is born of water and of the Spirit he cannot enter the Kingdom of God.*' Do either of you know what the Kingdom of God is?"

Memaw included both girls in the conversation, though Olivia never spoke.

"Hmm, Heaven?" asked Annette.

"Heaven is a place our spirits go to be with Jesus when we die until God establishes His physical Kingdom on Earth again. This will happen in the future when God will bring heaven to earth. Jesus will rule and reign here, and as believers, we will rule and reign with Him. That is a physical form of the Kingdom of God."

"But the Bible asks us to seek the Kingdom of God here on earth, now.[6] That means we're to pray and ask for Jesus to rule and reign in our lives now, to establish His Kingdom in our hearts so that Jesus can transform our lives.

Jesus said, '*For indeed, the Kingdom of God is within you.*'[7] When we ask Jesus to be Lord of our lives—not just our Savior, saving us from what we deserve for having sinned—but as Lord, we establish His Kingdom in our lives."

"When we live with Christ as Lord—we surrender control of our lives to Jesus, that is the Kingdom of God living in us."

---

[4] Ezekiel 36:25-27

[5] Ephesians 5:25-27

[6] Matthew 6:33

[7] Luke 17:20&21

"Nicodemus needed to be born again to later see the physical Kingdom of God established here on the Earth, and to have the Kingdom of God rule and reign in his life at that time. Then Jesus could be Lord over him, to lead him to do righteous things. And Nicodemus could share God's Gospel or 'Good News' with others."

Annette stopped and looked at Memaw, "So we're supposed to be born again, like Jesus told Nicodemus. Then we can rule and reign on this Earth with Jesus one day,[8] but also, so Jesus can be King over our lives right now."

Memaw beamed, "Exactly! You've got it."

Opening the front gate of the property as they returned from their walk, Memaw reached to hold Olivia's hand. Olivia pulled back, avoiding the gesture.

Annette remained silent a few minutes. Releasing Memaw's hand she ran straight for her daddy who was helping Papa work on the tractor.

From the kitchen window Andrea could see they'd returned. She walked out with a pitcher of iced tea and glasses for everyone.

Annette couldn't contain what she had learned and she told her daddy and Papa in one long sentence what Jesus told Nicodemus about being born again, and how we all should be washed clean by the Spirit of God.[9] And if we do that, we would live with the Kingdom of God in our lives today. And rule with Jesus when Earth becomes His Kingdom one day.

Andrea gave Memaw a wide-eyed look. "Wow!"

"I want to be born again like Nicodemus," said Annette.

---

[8] Revelation 20:4

[9] John 3:3

Memaw's vision blurred from tears of joy at her grand-daughter's understanding and request to have Jesus as her Lord and Savior.

Andrea whispered, "Thank You, Jesus."

Annette's daddy, John, lifted her up onto the tractor bringing her closer to him. He wanted to make sure Annette understood what she was asking for. "What exactly do you mean by that?"

"Well, I want Jesus to be my Lord and Savior now so that He lives in me and guides me, so that one day I will see Him and live in His real Kingdom here on Earth."

John smiled at Memaw and without words showed there was no denying Annette fully understood what she was asking for.

"We can definitely do that," John said.

Papa asked, "Olivia, would you like to pray, too?"

Olivia looked at the ground and shook her head no.

John hugged Annette tightly and spoke gently, "This is a prayer that simply tells Jesus you want to give Him your life. You ask Him to wash you with His Spirit and make you clean. It is a start to you living out your salvation as you learn His Word and get close to Him by reading the Bible. Close your eyes and say what I say."

Papa, Memaw, John and Andrea, all closed their eyes and touched Annette as an expression of extending their faith and agreement with her prayer. Olivia pretended not to pay attention, staring at the group.

Annette's daddy led her in a prayer.

"Heavenly Father, thank You for Jesus," John said and Annette repeated his words after each phrase.

"You teach us how to live and what we should do," they continued.

"I want to live each day with Jesus in me, leading me and guiding me to be like Him."

"Please forgive me for all the bad choices I have made."

A tear ran down Annette's cheek as she said the words.

"Please help me to show Jesus' love to others," she repeated.

"And to tell others of Jesus' love for them."

"Thank You, Father, in Jesus' name I pray."

When Annette looked up, she gave a sigh and it seemed a heavy weight had just been lifted from her.

Everyone except Olivia cheered and hugged her. They all wiped tears from their eyes.

John pulled her off the tractor and got down on one knee in front of his daughter. "Now Sweetheart, you have a responsibility to read the Bible and get intimately close with God so you can know how much He loves you and how you can share His love with others. That way you're living and loving others like He did."

"Let's find your brothers and sisters and tell them the great news!" Andrea said.

"I'm gonna make a cake in celebration of your birthday!" said Memaw.

"Wait, it's not her birthday, is it?" said Olivia.

"It's her spiritual birthday," Memaw said.

When the group broke up, Papa James stood at the tractor wiping away tears, praying silently his gratitude to God.

With head bowed Olivia walked onto the porch to sit in a chair by herself.

3.

PRAISE GOD AND WORSHIP BEFORE THE BATTLE

"Enter into His gates with thanksgiving, and into His courts with praise. Be thankful to Him, and bless His name."
Psalm 100:4

"Don't be sad, my babies, your daddy is going to be fine. The doctors are helping him," said Memaw.

"What if they can't help him?" asked Elizabeth.

"Let's pray and ask God to please give the doctors wisdom.[10] Gather around and hold each other's hands, bow your heads and close your eyes. I'll start the prayer and whoever wants to pray, start once I'm done. Let's begin by worshiping our Heavenly Father."[11]

"Why do we worship God before praying?" asked James.

"I'll explain afterwards; right now, we need to pray."

---

[10] James 1:5

[11] John 4:23-24

"Father, we worship and exalt Your name.[12] We praise the splendor of Your holiness.[13] You are worthy of praise.[14] We worship You, we give You thanks, we praise You for Your glory.[15] Bless You, Lord.[16] As the heavens and the flowers of the field and the mountains bow down, we bow in worship, as well.[17] Receive our praise. Thank You that You are Lord and Healer. As the children and I come before You, we ask for forgiveness for anything we may have said or done that did not glorify You and may have hurt others.[18] Bring to our remembrance anything we must repent of, or ask forgiveness for, Father, that we may approach Your Throne with a clean heart so our prayers going up for John will be heard.[19] We thank You for being such a forgiving Father.[20] We lift up the children's daddy, my son, and pray that You would be with him and that he'd know the love You have for him. We thank You for Your love, Lord. Please give the doctors wisdom[21] to know how to be able to help him quickly and effectively. Thank You that what the enemy intended for evil, You use for good.[22] Please comfort Andrea

---

[12] Psalm 34:3

[13] Psalm 96:9

[14] Revelation 4:11

[15] Psalm 150:6

[16] Psalm 103:1

[17] Psalm 95:6 & Psalm 96:11&12

[18] Psalm 66:18

[19] Psalm 24:3-5

[20] Matthew 6:14

[21] James 1:5

[22] Genesis 50:20

and the children. I proclaim there will be no fear.[23] Embrace the family with Your perfect love that casts out fear.[24] Thank You that Your perfect will[25] in this situation is that we'd walk as the healed of the Lord. That is one of the reasons You sent Your Precious Son to die on the cross for us.[26] Thank You for that Perfect Gift.[27] We receive His sacrifice of love and not allow it to have been for nothing. We receive the healing that comes from Jesus having shed His blood for us to have it.[28] Father, we thank You for it with grateful hearts."

Memaw remained silent a few moments so the children would pick up on it being their turn to pray.

James said, "Thank You, God, for our dad. We ask that dad's healing would happen quickly and that he could come home to us soon. Thank You, Jesus, for all you've done for us."

"Anyone else want to pray?" asked Memaw after a moment of silence.

"I do." said Annette. "Thank You Jesus that You take care of us and Mommy and Daddy. Please let Daddy be alright. Amen."

After a moment, Memaw concluded the prayer by saying, "Thank You for being here with us, for hearing our prayers,[29] Father, we pray all these things in agreement with each other,[30]

---

[23] Deuteronomy 31:6

[24] I John 4:18

[25] Mark 16:15-18

[26] I John 3:8

[27] James 1:17

[28] Isaiah 53:5 & 1 Peter 2:24

[29] 1 John 5:14 & Matthew 18:20

[30] Matthew 18:19

and in the name of Your Son, Jesus Christ, our Lord and Savior. Amen."[31]

"There. It's covered in prayer. We have to thank God for hearing our prayers and for the work He does on our behalf and rest in His peace that Daddy is alright."

Placing a hand on his shoulder Memaw said, "I can answer your question now, James. You'd asked why we worship God before praying. That's a good question."

She lifted a sleepy little Addy into her arms and sat on the rocker. Everyone listen and I'll tell you a story."

The children sprawled on the couch and the living room floor to hear. Memaw rocked little Addy to sleep in her arms.

Olivia was in the room, but sat away and apart from the group. Not because she wasn't invited, but she chose to sit separate. It's not likely she was taught to be quiet and respect a family's intimate moments; fact is, she needed to protect her feelings and not allow herself to care for or love this family, there would come a time that she leaves.

"Praise is an important part of our time with God. Worship is powerful.[32] The Bible tells us to, 'Come into His gates with thanksgiving and into His courts with praise.'[33] Anybody know what that means?"

"I do." said James with raised hand.

"Tell us."

"It's like we go into a place when we go to God in prayer."

"Yes, we do. It is a glorious place to be in God's presence. Unlike any other place, it's special. We have to enter into His

---

[31] John 14:13-14

[32] Psalm 95:1-7

[33] Psalm 100:4

presence as though we are going through a gate to get close to Him; we are entering the spiritual presence of the Most High God so we do that by worshiping Him with our words; with our hearts; with reverence; with joy; with praises that express to Him how much we love, honor, thank, adore and appreciate Him."

"God looks at the heart, just as in salvation. When you apologize, when you tell the truth, when you say things to 'help' someone, God looks at the motives in your heart to read your sincerity. He does the same to read your sincerity in your praises to Him. He knows if you're worshipping to impress another person, or to attempt to get Him to answer your prayer; or if you truly mean what you're saying and doing. His Word says, '...we must worship Him in spirit and in truth.'[34] You must always mean it very seriously from the heart when you worship Him, and He will know it otherwise. There is no place for pride in worship. We have to know God and believe all He saved us from to worship Him in truth."

"The Bible also tells us to approach the Throne of Grace with a gift.[35] What gifts could God possibly want from us?"

"Love?" asked Annette.

"Yes. That is a perfect gift to give God. Our love." said Memaw. "What else?"

"Obedience." said James.

"Absolutely. Obedience is a form of worship and shows Him our love. The Bible even says, obedience is better than sacrifice.[36] What else?"

---

[34] John 4:24

[35] Psalm 96:8 & Psalm 100:2

[36] 1 Samuel 15:22

Sitting up from a near sleep Addy said, "I can draw Him a picture."

"I know He would like that. It would be showing Him your love through talents He gave you; that is definitely a gift," smiled Memaw.

"Do you have an idea, Olivia?" she asked.

Olivia only nodded no.

"Our words of adoration and appreciation and reverence are all gifts to God.[37] When we speak those words to Him, we are gifting Him with praises and worshiping Him."

"What is admoration?" asked Annette.

"A-dor-a-tion." corrected Memaw. Adoration is respect, reverence, and devotion to God. Devotion is loyalty or being committed to God."

"Those are hard words," said Addy.

"Those are words grown-ups use. They should be used with reverence to God. It is definitely right to love your momma and daddy, and to show respect and obedience to them. But your love and respect and obedience to God should supersede the love and respect you show to anything, or anyone else." Memaw attempted to explain—finding it difficult to keep the explanation at a level the children could understand.

Elizabeth said, "God is an awesome God."

"Exactly!" said Memaw sitting back with satisfaction. "God is an awesome God. And that is adoration, praise and devotion. God is awesome. I couldn't have said it better myself."

What the faith of a child must do for God. Is it any wonder we are called to become as little children?[38]

---

[37] Malachi 1:11

[38] Matthew 18:3

"Back to our story. So, we know the Bible says to *enter His gates with thanksgiving and His courts with praise*.[39] As well, we're to *approach the Throne of God with a gift*,[40] of which we have decided the best gifts are words of adoration, reverence, devotion and love. Telling Him how awesome He is. And, using the talents He has given us such as drawing or painting, dancing, and playing music are all forms of worship."

"When we worship God with our praises and ask Him to come before us,[41] grown-ups call it 'ushering Him into our presence' or, inviting Him to spend time with us so that He can hear our praises and hear our prayers," said Memaw.

"God performs many miracles during worship. One of my favorite Bible stories is from 2 Chronicles where three armies, the Moabites, the Ammonites and the Meunites were headed toward Judah and Jerusalem to attack Jehoshaphat and his people."[42]

At this point, Uncle Daniel walked in with his children. "How's John doing?" he asked.

"We just prayed for him," said Memaw as she stood to hug and kiss the arriving grandchildren. "I'm telling the story of a battle from the Bible, please sit down and join us." Memaw sent the children to the living room as she answered Daniel about John in the kitchen.

"They're running tests. Andrea will call as soon as results are given. Your dad is outside in the shop, or you can join

---

[39] Psalm 100:4

[40] Psalm 150:1-6 & Romans 12:1

[41] James 4:8

[42] 2 Chronicles 20

us and listen about Jehoshaphat's enemies destroying themselves?" she smiled.

"I'll go say hi to Dad and leave you to the battle ground," winked Daniel, "then I'm heading out to the hospital to be with Andrea. Cynthia will meet us there. Where are the others?"

"Everyone's on their way. Some are heading straight to the hospital. Be safe and give Andrea our love. Tell her we're praying and not to worry about the children."

Daniel went out the side door reassuring his mom that John would be alright.

"Okay, now to get Ezra, Stephanie and Micah caught up. We're talking about inviting or ushering God into our presence with worship. We position ourselves to be heard by God in our prayers when we worship. You're just in time to hear of a battle."

"Cool." said Ezra at the thought of Memaw telling a story of armies fighting battles.

"Jehoshaphat heard word that armies of Moabites, Ammonites, and Meunites were headed toward Judah and Jerusalem to attack." Everyone's attention was now focused on Memaw's story of three armies coming against a small army.

"Jehoshaphat was afraid so he sought the Lord and proclaimed a fast throughout all Judah. Do you know what a fast is?" asked Memaw.

"It's like going on a diet, I think?" said Elizabeth.

"I can see why you'd think so, many people do stop eating certain foods when they fast, but going on a fast is to stop doing something or eating something in order to make yourself available to pray instead. When we fast for a day from eating food, during the time you would normally be eating, you pray instead."

"Some people fast from their phones, so instead of scrolling through social media, they spend that time praying. Others fast from a particular food such as all meat, or any candy, or sleeping, watching T.V., anything."

"During the time they would normally be doing something else, be it eating or watching T.V., they would instead, pray." she explained. "Fasting positions us to put aside distractions so that we hear from God."

"Jehoshaphat asked all the people of Judah and Jerusalem to stop eating and to, instead, pray to God for wisdom and direction. Then Jehoshaphat stood before all the people and prayed to the Lord their God saying, '*O Lord, You are the God of our fathers and the God in the heavens, are you not? And aren't you the Ruler over all kingdoms of the nations? All power and might are in Your hand, so that no one can stand against You.*' He was praising and worshipping God there. '*Will You not hear our distress now and deliver us, as You did our fathers? For we are powerless against this great multitude who are coming against us; nor do we know what to do, but our eyes are on You,*' he prayed."

"As all of Judah stood there with their wives, babies and children listening to Jehoshaphat pray, the Spirit of the Lord came upon Jahaziel and asked him to say, '*Listen, all people who live in Judah and Jerusalem; listen King Jehoshaphat, thus says the Lord to you all: Do not be afraid or dismayed because of the great multitude, for the battle is not yours, but God's.*' Jahaziel told them all, '*Tomorrow go down against them.*' "

"God told them exactly where the enemies would be. Jahaziel said, '*They will come up near Ziz and you will find them at the end of the valley in front of the wilderness of Jeruel. You don't need to fight them in this battle. Just position yourselves. Stand and see Me do the work on your behalf, O Judah and Jerusalem. Do not fear or be stressed about it. Tomorrow, go out and face them, for I am with you.'* " she said dramatically. "Jehoshaphat bowed with his face to the ground before God, and all Judah and the people of Jerusalem fell down to worship Him. Then the Levites stood and began praising the Lord God of Israel with loud voices," for a moment Memaw bowed her head in silence and reverence to God.

"Then what happened?" asked David.

"Did they fight?" Micah asked.

"I'll bet God put out His sword and smote them all!" reenacted Elizabeth.

"Even better," went on Memaw, "Let me explain."

"They got up early the next morning and went to the wilderness and Jehoshaphat stood out in front of them and said, *'Listen to me, O Judah and people of Jerusalem, put your trust in the Lord your God and you will be taken care of.'* After Jehoshaphat had spoken this to the people, he had the Levites go out in front of the army and told them, *'Begin to sing praises and worship to God. Give thanks to the Lord, for His loving kindness is forever.'* When they began singing and praising, the Lord set ambushes against the armies of Ammon, Moab and Mount Seir. They changed directions from where they were originally heading. It ended up being that the armies of Ammon and Moab turned and attacked and completely destroyed the army of Mount Seir. When they finished destroying that army, they turned on each other and destroyed one another, the Ammonites against the Moabites."

"Agghhhh!"

"Whooaaa!"

"Wow!" began the children in simultaneous cheering and awe at what the Lord had done to Judah and Jerusalem's enemies.

"Did Jehoshaphat's army never fight at all?" asked Olivia. Memaw smiled. She was actually listening.

"No, they didn't have to. He and his army came up to the lookout of the wilderness and they looked toward where the fighting had been and there were only dead soldiers lying about on the ground. No one had escaped."

"That's sad," whispered Stephanie.

"That is very sad, but a good reminder to you all to be careful whose side you're on. You'd better stay on God's side with the righteous and not end up being an enemy of God's, nor of His people." She took advantage of the opportunity to encourage the children to never leave the narrow path.

"Is that all?" asked Micah.

"Well, only that Jehoshaphat and his people did go down to the battle ground and gather the spoils. They collected so much it took them three days to carry it all away."

"What are spoils?" asked David.

"Spoils are the valuables left behind by the armies that died in battle. It was the people of Judah and Jerusalem that got to keep it all. After three days of carrying all the clothes, goods, and valuables left behind, on the fourth day, the people gathered to do what? Can anybody guess?"

"They thanked God, I hope." said Stephanie.

"They sure did. They came together with much gladness and joy with harps, lyres and trumpets to praise and worship the Lord God who saved them from their enemies."

"So, the answer to James' original question of why we should worship before prayer. Can anyone tell me what you learned from this story that answers that?" asked Memaw.

"I can."

"Tell us, James."

"Well, to usher God into our presence to hear our prayers we must worship Him first."

"Is that the only time God hears our prayers, do you suppose? After we've worshiped Him?" asked Memaw.

"I hope not. Sometimes we have emergency prayers," said David.

"No, you're right David, we don't always have time for long worship, but when telling God how much we love Him and how wonderful He is becomes a standard part of our prayers, it becomes automatic to include it. And, we don't only worship when we pray. True worship is constant. We should be thinking of Him and worshipping Him in all we do and say all day long."

"This Bible story is an example of what I meant when I said that miracles happen during worship. The enemies defeated themselves without Judah and Jerusalem ever having to go into battle because they worshiped first. That was definitely a miracle. The Bible clearly says, the miracle happened during the time they were worshiping."

"Let's not forget that approaching the Throne of God with gifts of praise and worship is a big part of Him hearing our prayers. It's not to bribe God into giving us what we ask for in our prayers. It's out of love, adoration and devotion to Him that we offer our praises and worship to Him because of who He is, not because of what we want from Him."

"Do you know what the Bible says if we don't praise Him?" Without waiting for an answer, "That the stones will cry out to Him." [43]

"Yes, when Jesus came into Jerusalem riding a donkey colt, the people welcomed him by spreading their coats on the

---

[43] Luke 19:40

road to reverence Him and show that they would rather have Jesus on his donkey, trample their coats than to have Him walk through the mud and the mire on the street." [44]

"As he entered the city, the crowd and the disciples were singing joyful praises and worshiping Him for all the miracles he had made happen."

"The Pharisees didn't like this behavior much, so they asked him, 'Teacher, rebuke your disciples for shouting and behaving in such a manner.' "

"But Jesus answered them, 'I'll tell you instead. If these people stop and become silent, the stones will cry out to me." [45]

"So you see, we should cry out our praises to God," she encouraged.

"So that the rocks won't have to," Stephanie said.

"That's right, so that the rocks won't have to," laughed Memaw, "but also because Jesus said that those who love Him will keep His commandments. [46] If we say we love and worship Him, but do not obey Him, our worship is worthless. We must obey His Word and live like Jesus did."

"Come on guys, let's have a battle!" said David. "You be the Ammonites, Micah, Olivia and Elizabeth. James, Stephanie and Annette, you are the Moabites. Ezra and Addy, you're with me, I'm Jehoshaphat!"

All the children began their rendition of the battle as Ezra, Addy and David began to sing, "God is so good. God is so good. God is so good, He's so good to me. We love Him so..."

---

[44] Luke 19:35&36

[45] Luke 19:37-40

[46] John 14:15

Memaw left them to their battle and went to start supper. The phone rang. "Andrea, I'm so happy you called. How is John?"

"He's awake and doing much better. He suffered a concussion and has some bleeding on the brain, which is what is causing the severe headache, but he's gonna to be alright, thank God," she explained.

"Glory be to God the Father. Hallelujah." said Memaw. "What an answer to prayer. Thank You, Jesus!"

"Yes, Momma, thanks to Jesus," said Andrea. "They're going to keep him for observation to monitor him and be sure the pain doesn't get excruciating."

"Understandably," replied Memaw. "That is best, I'm certain. Please don't worry about the children. They are fine, playing with their cousins and Olivia. Is Daniel with you now?"

"Yes, Ma'am. He arrived shortly before the doctor came in. Luke and Lisa, are here as well and the others are on their way, they've texted and called. Laura and Ethan are bringing food. Thank you for everything. I'll be in touch and please kiss the kids for me."

Hanging up the phone, Memaw walked back into the living room. "It appears God has already answered your prayers, children. Momma called to report your daddy is doing much better." she said with warmth in her heart and a smile on her face. "Thank You, Jesus."

4.

ALWAYS BE READY

"Therefore you also be ready, for the Son of Man
is coming at an hour you do not expect."
Matthew 24:44

Matthew huffed out the back door letting the screen door slam extra hard. He picked up the ax Papa James kept in the barn and turned toward the stump. Without standing a log, Matthew went at the stump as though he were trying to split the chopping block itself.

"Who makes the...*chop*...first string quarterback...*chop*...sit out training camp...*chop*...because of one dumb...*chop*...piece of paper?"

He wiped the sweat from his brow and yelled, "Isn't it a given he should be at football camp?"

He put the ax down. No one heard him, but he felt better.

Memaw and Olivia watched from the kitchen. Memaw matched his rhythmic swings at the stump by punching the dough.

"Why is Matthew so mad?" asked Olivia.

"I don't know, Honey. Let's pray for him." With floury hands Memaw grabbed Olivia's hands and began praying. Olivia wasn't sure what to do or say, but she bowed her head and closed her eyes.

When the bread dough was ready, she placed it in an oiled bowl and covered it with a cotton dish towel and left it to rise. Then she poured three tall glasses of iced lemonade.

She said to Olivia, "Here, you take him the lemonade."

They walked out to Matthew and found him sitting on the chopping block. His head in his hands, the ax lay at his feet.

"Cold lemonade?" said Memaw and Olivia extended the glass.

"I'm good," Matthew said, red-faced and sweaty.

He had never turned down a cold lemonade before.

"Whatever it is, remember, God's got your back." Memaw encouraged.

Matthew scowled, "Can He miraculously turn back the clock?"

"Why would you want that?"

He picked up a rock and threw it at the barn. "So I can turn in the signed permission form for Training Camp."

"What happened?"

"I didn't turn in the permission slip by the deadline."

She ran a finger down the side of the glass, leaving a line in the water forming on the outside. "Well, I guess they have a reason for the rules. Just like in the game, right?"

"It's a dumb rule."

"But you can't pick and choose the rules you want to follow. What do they call it when a player grabs another one when they're running to catch a pass?"

"Interference?"

"That's it," Memaw said. "The rules apply to everybody evenly. To keep things fair."

"Shouldn't they make an exception for the starting quarterback? I need to be there. How are they supposed to practice the plays without me? They can't."

Memaw took a deep breath. "They will, Matthew. Whether it feels wrong or not, they'll find a way."

"I know." Matthew threw another rock. "That's what hurts most. They don't need me, Memaw. What if I lose my position? What if Danny gets better than me? What if..." His voice trailed and he shook his head. "All because of a dumb piece of paper."

"Is it really about the paper?"

"Yes, It's so stupid! It should be automatic that I'm there. How could I not be?"

"I'm sorry, Mijo." she answered, using an endearing Spanish word meaning 'my son'. She placed her hand on his balled-up fist. "I can't help but think of something the Bible talks about."

"The Bible talks about Football Training Camp?"

"No, but the way you're feeling reminds me of how some people might react after the Rapture. Many will feel angry at being left behind, at not being caught up in the air to go with Jesus."[47]

He dug a toe in the dirt.

Olivia came out from behind a tree and sat on a nearby trailer bed.

"Matthew, I know you feel devastated for missing out on the training camp. And it may cost you playing time. I can't argue with that."

---

[47] Luke 21:36

He looked at her with a scowl. "This is supposed to make me feel better?"

"I don't just want to make you feel better. I want you to get a different perspective. Our choices can cost us. And I don't want you to merely learn to turn in permission slips on time. There's a valuable lesson here. Every choice to do, or not do something will have consequences. Some are more costly than others. Some won't have much effect. But the greatest choice you can make is to receive Jesus as Savior and live for Him."

"I know that, Memaw."

"I know you do, but imagine what life would look like if the people you love and trust, and count on weren't there. The people you go to when you're hurting. You are so blessed, Mijo. Your family and friends love you. But what if those people were suddenly gone? Who would be there for you? Who would help pay for your college? Let's be honest, your grades aren't exactly..."

"Memaw, I do have Jesus as my Savior and Lord. Why are you telling me this?"

Memaw stood from the bale of hay and faced him. She said a silent prayer, asking God to touch him with her words. "Two reasons. Yes, you do have Jesus as your Savior, but put yourself in the shoes of those who don't. Do you realize what the world will look like after followers of Christ are Raptured?"[48]

"Think about it. Satan has always wanted to rule like God. The Tribulation is his opportunity to rule the world through the Anti-Christ, until Jesus comes back to defeat him.[49] And at some point, during the last half of those seven years Satan, himself,

---

[48] Matthew 24:21

[49] Revelation 13

will come to earth. The Bible says the first three and a half years will be bad, but not as horrific and dreadful as the last three and a half years. The Book of Revelation speaks of there being earthquakes, hail storms with fire and blood, famine, darkness, terrible things." [50]

"That sounds horrible."

"It will be. And compared to your circumstance with the team, it puts it into perspective, doesn't it?"

"But those are such different levels of situations. I didn't follow through with a paper, but the consequences for not following Jesus..." He looked at the ground and a cloud came over him. "All I have to go through is a week of no training camp. You can't compare the two."

Memaw smiled and sat again, putting an arm around his shoulder. "You're right. So now you have a better perspective. You missing camp doesn't feel like the end of the world."

He took a deep breath, "Ahh, Memaw. I guess not."

They sat in silence together. Olivia sat on the trailer listening to every word but never spoke.

Matthew asked, "What happens to the people who thought they would be raptured because they acknowledge Jesus and do good things, but missed the boat for being lukewarm?" [51]

"Many good people will be left behind who thought they were Christians. Some will probably resent that they didn't get raptured. They may blame God and turn against Him and end up separated from Him forever. Or, because God made provision for them even after the Rapture, [52] those people may

---

[50] Revelation 6

[51] Matthew 7:21-23 & Revelation 3:16

[52] Revelation 7:9-14

commit their lives fully during the Tribulation. But the Bible says they will be martyred for their commitment to Christ.[53] Do you realize how difficult life will be with Satan, the Anti-Christ and the False Prophet ruling the earth?"[54]

Matthew turned to her, "You said there were two reasons you were telling me this. What's the other?"

"Glad you asked, Mijo," Memaw stood again, "the other is, don't ever get so caught up with life that you forget to live out the Great Commission. It's so important to share the Gospel with friends, neighbors and family that might miss out on living like Jesus and the eternal life God promises."

"I've never given it much thought," he admitted.

"Don't forget what it will be like for those left behind."

"I do kind of live my life thinking, 'I'm set'. I don't usually consider what not sharing the Gospel message with others will look like. You've given me a lot to think about. Thank you."

"I'm glad you see this is not the end of your football world. And that you've been reminded of the importance of sharing with others the way to have eternal life with Jesus, but also how to live like Jesus here and now. And maybe you've learned more about being responsible for what needs to get accomplished today and to follow the rules that have been given."

"Yeah. I guess it's my fault for missing the deadline. I need to stay on top of important stuff—like giving my truck insurance money to Dad on time each month." Could you give me a ride to Peter's house? I have to let him and Coach know I'm not going to camp. And then, have a serious sit-down talk about a boat he could miss."

---

[53] Matthew 24:9

[54] Revelation 13

Memaw smiled, "Sure, let me get my keys. But first, you need to drink your glass of lemonade."

She reached out to Olivia and they walked back to the house together, Memaw's arm around her shoulder. When they made it to the porch Olivia turned and saw Matthew still on the stump holding an empty glass.

Memaw and Olivia drove Matthew to Peter's house. He said, "Thank you, Memaw, for everything. Bye Olivia." Stepping out of the car he opened Olivia's back door so she could move up to the front seat. He touched her shoulder, made eye contact and said, "Hope you've surrendered your life to Jesus, Olivia. If not, please consider getting serious about it soon."

Memaw smiled.

On the drive home Olivia said, "You always make everything about Jesus when you talk to your grandchildren."

"You're right. Because that is what God created us for. We're not put on this earth to live life for ourselves. We're to live out Jesus' love toward others like He would love them and serve them. Yes, we have to live life here on this Earth by working, playing, learning. But as we go along doing life it should be with the sole purpose of living out God's love toward others. At least, that's what God's intention is according to the Bible.[55] Whether people actually do that, or not, is determined by whether we are living for Him, or for ourselves."

"I don't get it. We can't live for ourselves? We have to live for others?"

"Not exactly. We have to live for Christ. It's not a rule, as much as a truth we should instinctively live by when we are

---

[55] 1 John 5:1&2

saved. We don't live by it because of Adam and Eve's sin," said Memaw, then explained.

"You see, God created a perfect world and placed Adam and Eve in His perfect world to live in and take care of it.[56] The devil approached them in the form of a snake and deceived them into thinking they would be like God if they ate the fruit from the tree of Knowledge of Good and Evil."[57]

Memaw was rejoicing over the opportunity to share this precious story with Olivia.

"Eve told the devil, *'But God told us not to eat it or we would surely die.'*[58]

She imitated the snake, "*'Surely, you will not die, on the contrary, you will be like God, you will know good from evil,'*[59] the snake told her."

"Eve looked at the fruit and saw how beautiful it was and was deceived into believing it couldn't possibly hurt to eat it and it would make her be like God, so she bit into it and gave it to Adam to eat, too.[60] That disobedience to God is what caused the fall of man. From that moment on sin came upon man in many forms from selfishness and greed, to lust and bad thoughts, to murder and stealing, and many other ways. Have you ever heard that story?" asked Memaw.

"Yes, but I never understood what it meant and how it affects us today. How could something that happened so long ago affect us today?"

---

[56] Genesis 1:26-30

[57] Genesis 1:4&5

[58] Genesis 1:3

[59] Genesis 1:4&5

[60] Genesis 1:6

"Well, after Adam and Eve had children and the population of the earth grew, and because of sin having entered the world, people needed a way to be forgiven of their sin. So, they would take perfect animals such as a lamb, bull, goat, or bird to priests in temples to kill and offer them to God as a sacrifice for their sins.[61] But it was a sacrifice that would temporarily restore the relationship between God and humanity. A more perfect and lasting sacrifice was needed that was permanent, not having to be done over and over again."

"Jesus?" asked Olivia.

"That's right. Jesus was the perfect, once for all sacrifice.[62] God came in the form of Jesus.[63] He made Himself to be born of a woman so that He would know and understand all of mankind's temptations and overcame them all to help us when we get tempted."[64]

"I think I get it," Olivia said.

"Good. So back to your original question of, 'why can't we live for ourselves.' We actually live sinfully until the moment we surrender our lives completely so that God can transform us into being His children to manifest Him."[65]

"What does *manifest Him* mean?" asked Olivia.

"To manifest Christ is to behave like Christ, treat others like He would, love like He does."

"But no one is perfect," said Olivia.

---

[61] Leviticus 22:17-33

[62] Hebrews 10:1-18

[63] John 1:14

[64] Hebrews 2:18

[65] Ephesians 2:1-10

"That's what the world likes to say, more so to justify why they're not acting like Jesus, I think," said Memaw, turning on her windshield wipers as the drizzle got heavier.

"While we may never be perfect, we are to strive to be like Jesus."[66]

"When we *try* to keep from sinning, and we *try* to change, and we *try* to be good and we fail, we blame Him for not helping us. Jesus never expected us to be good by ourselves. He said, we are to give ourselves completely and entirely over to Him and Holy Spirit does the work in us.[67] That is what the Bible calls, dying to self and picking up our cross."[68]

"If more people truly understood that it is impossible—we cannot, in and of ourselves, transform ourselves. Only Holy Spirit can transform us. And when we allow Him to, it is a complete work. When we try by ourselves, it is a failed work."

With a confused look Olivia asked, "I'm lost again. How do we die to ourselves and what does that thing about picking up a cross mean?"

"Remember when we were on our walk with Annette and I told the story about Jesus telling Nicodemus he needs to get born-again? And how that didn't actually mean going into his mother's womb to come out a second time. It meant, to have the Kingdom of God rule and reign in his life he needs Jesus to be Lord over his life by dying to himself and becoming born again?"

"Ohhh, yes okay, I get it." Olivia's face lit up as she made the connection.

---

[66] 1 John 2:6

[67] 1 Corinthians 6:11

[68] Matthew 16:24

"Good. Now, picking up your cross is like when Jesus picked up and had to carry his own cross to his death place. We, knowing we need to die to ourselves, need to carry our cross to Jesus and allow Him to make us new again or, born-again."

"It's easy to understand when you explain it," Olivia said.

"And that is the reason the Bible says we should make disciples of new, born-again believers.[69] A disciple is a follower of Christ. Disciples need to know about Christ and the Word of God to be able to follow Christ and what His Word says. Unfortunately, many people are not getting discipled."

Memaw concentrated going through the town's only intersection and when completely through it asked, "You're familiar with the Bible story of Adam and Eve and knew that Jesus was the final sacrifice for us all, do you know Jesus as your Lord and Savior?"

"I thought I did. There was a family I lived with that said they were Christians but they didn't ever talk about Jesus, or go to church, or read their Bible. They sure didn't treat me like Jesus would treat me if you say Christians are supposed to treat others like Jesus would."

"Why would you say you thought you did and question it now?" asked Memaw.

"Because I didn't know any of what you've talked about with Annette or Matthew. The foster mom just told me if I wanted to go to Heaven when I died, I needed to say a prayer, so I did."

"I see."

"So, am I born-again?" asked Olivia.

---

[69] Matthew 28:19-20

"I can't say one way or the other because that's not for me to determine—only Jesus knows. I do know that God knows the intention of your heart when you prayed to Him. He knows whether or not you were sincere and genuine in your asking Him to save you."

Without waiting for a response Memaw continued, "But I want you to understand a very important fact. The most important reason to be born-again is to get the Kingdom of Heaven living in us now so that we know how to shine for Jesus in this sin-filled world today. So that we know how to love people. How to live forgiven and rid of your old self and live as a new person in Christ."

"Yes, those who are born-again will go to Heaven when we die an earthly death,[70] but having Heaven in us today is what determines how we live out this life while on earth."

"When we shine for Jesus, we are manifesting Christ and His righteousness so other people desire to shine for Him too. Is all of this making sense, Olivia?"

"I think so."

"Would you like to surrender your life to Jesus and ask Him to transform your life right now to be sure you are born-again?"

Olivia fiddled with the seatbelt strap and bit her lip.

"You can go to Jesus yourself whenever you are ready. And if you feel like you've already surrendered your life to Him but aren't sure if the transformation has begun, ask Him to transform you. Trust Him. He loves you greatly, Sweetie. Talk to Jesus and ask Him what He would have you do," smiled Memaw. "He'll answer you."

---

[70] John 3:16

5.

FUN ISN'T ALWAYS GOOD

"And have no fellowship with the unfruitful works of darkness,
but rather expose them."
Ephesians 5:11

"*I* can't outrun you two, you're too fast!" exclaimed Memaw, as she collapsed on the trampoline catching her breath. Having been tagged by Olivia first and then her grandson, she was wiped out.

The three of them laughed together lying on their backs, breathing heavily, resting up for Memaw to tag them back.

"Memaw, Momma is your daughter, right?" questioned six-year-old Gabriel.

"Yup."

"So, you are her parent."

"Yup."

"Theeen, can you please tell her and Dad to let us dress up and go trick or treating? They won't let us go. If you tell them, they have to listen to you and obey their parent," Gabriel asked with hope.

"It doesn't work that way anymore, Gabriel. Yes, I am your mommy's momma, but I no longer have authority over her to tell her what to do. She is an adult and no longer needs to listen to Papa's and my rule. She does what your daddy and her feel is best for you."

Gabriel lay there silent and thoughtful with a look of disappointment and defeat. He thought this plan would work and it failed.

"Sweetheart, this might disappoint you, but I agree with your daddy and your momma's decision in not allowing you and your siblings to dress up and go trick-or-treating."

Gabriel sat up sharply and looked at Memaw. With shock and a touch of offense he asked, "Why? It is so much fun dressing up and getting candy. And if we go to Sam's church, we're safe. It's not like we're going to be walking in a dangerous place where someone could hurt us. We'll be at a church. Our church should put on something like this. We'd be ministering to so many children in a safer place than the streets."

"We do believe in reaching the community with ministry and outreach events. We could minister to others walking into their environment of evil having prayed ourselves up, having put on the full armor of God,[71] having others covering us in prayer during the time we're in the battlefield; but hosting an event as an alternative to Halloween, means preparing the evil environment to then minister in. You would actually be participating with all the evils of Halloween and everything it stands for. From the costumes, to the candy, to the games, and doing it under the cover of night. In doing all that, you're opening the

---

[71] Ephesians 6:11-18

door for evil to enter the grounds and hearts of all involved. Do you see the dangers?" explained Memaw.

"How is it dangerous?" pouted Gabriel. This just wasn't going as planned at all. He sat looking at his hands, not even wanting to look at Memaw.

Even Olivia sat straight up on the trampoline to listen. She's participated with Halloween activities all her life at each foster home she was in. She thought scary costumes were frightening, but not evil.

It is not easy to critique as positively as one can something the church, or any entity, sees as fun for kids and a safe alternative to something dangerous or evil. Memaw carefully chose her words as she didn't want to condemn, but merely state her position and defend Gabriel's parents' decision.

"Gabriel," she sat up and spoke very seriously to him, "the traditions followed through with at these Halloween alternative events, under the guise of community outreach, all have evil pagan roots just as Halloween itself is based on."[72]

Gabriel wanted to know why it was bad, but didn't want to hear that it was bad. He was torn. He wants to have fun with all his friends. How could something at a church possibly be evil? It was at a church for goodness' sake. Everything done at churches should be safe and harmless. *I just wish someone would understand,* he thought.

With this war waging inside of him, he worked hard at staying respectful with his tone as he asked, "How is it evil, and what are pagan roots?" he grumbled.

"I'm glad you want to know, Honey. I know this is hard for you to understand, but you have to trust your parents'

---

[72] Deuteronomy 18:9-14

judgment.[73] And maybe you should ask them, too, but I'll do my best at explaining why Papa James and I didn't allow your momma and tias and tios to participate."

"When I say having 'pagan roots' it means the traditions of a group of people that have more than one god. They don't believe in the One and Only true God.[74] So their rituals, or traditions they participate with are all part of worshiping their many gods."

Suddenly Gabriel felt the realization of what this might actually mean. His facial expression changed and his demeanor softened and he looked at Memaw as if to say, 'go on' but didn't say a word.

"To give out candy today mimics the druids giving 'treats' to the souls of the dead that went about haunting people on this night playing 'tricks.' If the souls of the dead were treated, they would not play tricks—or cast spells on the people," she explained.

Knowing she had his attention she continued, "Dressing up in costumes started with people believing ghosts would come out at night on October 31st. To escape the evil spirits, they would wear costumes so the evil spirits would think they were a ghost, too, and not a live human so that no spells would be cast on them. Others believed they could take on the spirit of the animal they dressed up as. When I researched the meaning of everything, there were so many different religious rituals done in different parts of the world by different groups that there is more than one reason for doing the celebrations and traditions that were done. It just depends on what time in history and who

---

[73] Ephesians 6:1-3

[74] Exodus 34:14

was doing the celebrating. But it all related and added up to one common denominator—evil."

"I hope you see and understand that while many people, even some Christians, say it is harmless to wear a costume of a Bible figure or a cute little animal—as long as it is not a scary costume, it's okay. It really isn't. You are still participating with a tradition whose meaning had evil intentions behind it. It is not the scariness of the costume that matters, it's the meaning behind the dressing up, that matters."

"And jack-o-lanterns. The carving of pumpkins began with a story about a man named Jack who wasn't allowed to enter heaven because of his stinginess. He could not enter Hell because he had played jokes on the devil. So, he had to walk the earth with his lantern until Judgment Day. Now is that the way Christians believe?" asked Memaw.

Gabriel only nodded 'no' as he sat in shock over the magnitude of the evil behind what he was asking for.

"Christians like to say putting lights inside a carved pumpkin represents Jesus being the shining light inside us. However, to actually participate in carving out a pumpkin and creating a lantern in the same way Jack did, knowing full well what it represented, is entirely different. You can't participate with something you knowingly know is evil and justify it by making up a cute story to change its meaning. God is not mocked."

"Wow." was all Gabriel could say. He was taking it all in and learning about something that could have otherwise hurt him and jeopardized his soul.

Olivia didn't realize the repercussions to her soul; however, she was learning how every part of the holiday represents such evil.

Memaw took advantage of her captive audience and continued with the descriptive evils, "The Romans held 'Harvest Festivals' to honor Pamona, the goddess of fruit and trees. Bobbing for apples comes from this worship. "What did you say your friend's church called their festival you want to go to?"

"A 'Harvest Festival'," he answered with big eyes.

"And what time of day do all these events take place, I mean both now on Thursday at this church and back then when they worshiped doing these things?"

"At night," he answered, no longer sure. What he thought to be in the name of fun, actually took on an entirely different meaning.

"Yes, all these events are usually done in the darkness of night.[75] The word 'darkness' is mentioned 158 times in the Bible. Almost always darkness, and things done in darkness relate to evil."[76]

"October 31st is the time when registered witch covens meet to practice their worship of Satan. In an interview, a former Witch of Europe, wrote that the satanists loved the way Christians participate in their rituals. Do you still want to participate in what you thought was just fun at church on that night?"

"Pshh, no."

"Honey, in Thessalonians the Bible says, 'we are to abstain from all appearance of evil'.[77] By putting on an event on or around Halloween defines participating with Halloween and the evils of the devil."

---

[75] Ephesians 5:11

[76] John 3:20

[77] 1 Thessalonians 5:22

"It is great for churches to put on outreach events to minister to the community, yes. But we should do them at any other
time of year other than on or around October 31ˢᵗ. That way, the
children and adults who attend are more receptive to the ministering you have planned to happen in addition to the added fun,
games and candy. Whereas on Halloween night, the children
are primarily there for the fun, games and candy first—just like
the majority of children across the nation that night."

"Of course, parents of the community will have their children there at a church on Halloween night. They may be lost,
but they love their children and want what is best and safest for
their children. But is the church effectively teaching 'have no
participation with evil' when the church is the one preparing
the evil environment for them?"

She continued, "We, as followers of Christ, are to be the
salt—be different than the world, standout and be strong.[78] We
are to teach to choose and do the right thing, especially at the
expense of having fun.[79] If we can be trusted to say 'no' to a
little fun, we can be girded, strong and armed to say 'no' to
bigger temptations."[80]

"Above all else, Gabriel and Olivia, learn this: We are to
be like Jesus in everything we do and everything we say.[81]
Would Jesus have participated with dressing up in costumes
and handing out candy to have people listen to what He had to
say? To offer to heal them? To offer to pray for them? We are
not Jesus, Himself, but we are supposed to be like Him and do

---

[78] Matthew 5:13

[79] Romans 13:14

[80] Luke 16:10

[81] 1 Corinthians 10:31

as He would do and say as He would say. Likewise, not do what He wouldn't, and not speak as He wouldn't. His Word tells us that *whoever says he abides in Him must walk in the same way in which He walked.*[82] Also that *everyone who has this hope fixed on Him purifies himself, just as He is pure."*[83]

"It is so sad and scary how the devil uses fun to entice us,"[84] said Olivia.

"Oh, he doesn't play fair,"[85] agreed Memaw. "What's worse, he convinces Christians we're doing a good thing."

Memaw gave an example, "It's like a church having an outreach to minister to the gamblers of a community. Should they set up poker tables and slot machines to attract the community gamblers to then hand out a tract that says, 'Jesus loves you, so you shouldn't participate with the evils of gambling'? We shouldn't participate and contribute to the wrong-doing to reach those doing wrong."

The Apostle Paul said, *'Do not be conformed to the ways of the world, but be transformed by the renewing of your mind, so that you may prove what the will of God is, that which is good and acceptable and perfect.'*[86] Paul also said, *'light has no fellowship with darkness.' "*[87]

"Now I see why Momma and Dad won't let us go to Sam's church for their Harvest Festival. I'm sorry I was mad," he confessed.

---

[82] 1 John 2:6

[83] 1 John 3:3

[84] Romans 12:21

[85] Luke 4:1-13

[86] Romans 12:2

[87] Ephesians 5:11

"It's okay, Mijo, it's hard to always understand why your parents make the choices and decisions they do. It's even hard for us as God's children to know and understand His ways. 'Your ways are not My ways'[88] He says in His Word."

"That is why God placed your parents in authority over you to help grow you and guide you. But that authority changes when you become an adult. Just like I no longer have authority over your momma, she and your dad will no longer have this authority over you one day. We can only pray that all the good we teach our children will stick and that you will make good choices when you're on your own. I'm sure proud of the choice your parents made not to let you participate with evil," she smiled hugging Gabriel.

"Yeah, I guess I am, too," said Gabriel. "I just have one more question," looking up at Memaw with concern.

"Shoot."

"How do I tell Sam what his church is doing is wrong?"

"Good question. Maybe instead of telling him his church is wrong, you just tell him the truth about why you can't go. Share with him the meanings of all the activities and dressing up, as you just learned. You can definitely pray that wisdom from Holy Spirit would fall upon the church leaders and they'd know what to do about such an event on October 31st," suggested Memaw.

"Pray and ask God what your part is. Perhaps you could suggest that together, Sam and his momma do a search on the internet of what the meaning of Halloween really is. It's all there. In the meantime, let's pray right now that the truths

---

[88] Isaiah 55:8&9

would be revealed to them[89] and they would come to the realization that under a different guise, they are still participating with all activities related to evil."

"Okay."

"And Gabriel, if your friends and their church choose to continue to participate with this. You can't criticize or judge them.[90] That's not for you to do. Only Jesus is Judge.[91] You stay loving them and praying for them."

"Yes ma'am."

"Thank you, Sweetheart," said Memaw. "Now let's pray for them and then get off this trampoline, I've gotta get supper started."

"But it was your turn to tag us," said Olivia.

"Yeah," joined Gabriel.

"All the more reason to stop now—I won!" she laughed.

"Hey, how's that so?" Gabriel and Olivia looked at each other disappointed the game was over and that Memaw declared herself the winner.

Laughing, she reached for their hands to pray.

---

[89] John 8:32

[90] Matthew 7:1-5

[91] James 4:12

6.

SUBMISSION AND TRANSFORMATION

"For God did not appoint us to wrath, but to obtain salvation through our Lord Jesus Christ, who died for us, that whether we wake or sleep, we should live together with Him."
1 Thessalonians 5:9-10

Olivia sat with her math book lying open on the table though she couldn't concentrate enough to work through any of the problems. *How awkward to be listening in as she cries,* she thought.

Stephanie sat beside Memaw on the living room sofa sniffling and wiping tears. She was handed tissues from the end table.

"Why did God allow Joe to get leukemia? He's just a kid," asked Stephanie sinking into Memaw's arms, exhausted from crying. "Why do bad things have to happen to good people?"

"Honey, I think that's the wrong question to ask. The Bible says the sun and the rain fall on the just and the unjust."[92] It's not that God decided Joe should get leukemia." She wiped Stephanie's face. "We live in a fallen world where Satan was handed the authority and dominion that was originally given to mankind. Unless we are redeemed back to our Father can we obtain that dominion and authority back from him. Satan attacks. He doesn't play fair. He wants to steal, kill and destroy as many as possible."[93]

"I believe that it doesn't too much matter why people get sick or have calamities happen. I know that God didn't make people sick. And whether they are because of the devil's doing; consequences of their own choices; or simply from living in a fallen world[94]–it could even be a true accident that causes the tragedy. It's not my place to say, guess, assume, nor presume to know why bad things happen," said Memaw.

"What I do know is that God desires that we'd be healed and whole.[95] He wouldn't have sent His Son to die a horrible death on the Cross if not.[96] I do believe that God does still heal today.[97] I trust Him with our bodies, our finances, our lives. I only believe what His Word says. Beyond that, I leave out the guessing altogether as to whether He will, or not; or when He will. That's not for me to know or decide. That's His job. I only

---

[92] Matthew 5:45

[93] John 10:10

[94] John 10:10

[95] Mark 16:17&18

[96] Isaiah 53:5

[97] Psalm 103:3

believe He can, and desires it for us. Whether it happens, or not, does not move my belief in whether He can, does, or will."

"I don't know Joe's situation, nor can I pretend to know why he's sick—that's not my place. Nevertheless, it still holds true that ultimately, no matter the reasoning for the trial in Joe's life, God will not leave us to walk through any bad situation alone when we ask Him to be with us."[98]

"God said we would have trouble in this world.[99] Troubles will come.[100] We will suffer.[101] Satan goes around like a roaring lion seeking whom he may devour.[102] That's when you submit to God, resist the devil and the devil will flee."[103]

"God sent His Son to give life and give it abundantly.[104] He sends blessings that come and overtake us. He causes our enemies that rise up against us to depart from us in seven different ways. The Lord commands blessings upon us and upon all we set our hands to do. He establishes us as His holy people." The quoting of scripture continued.

"He makes us abound in prosperity—not my words, His Words—and prosperity doesn't only mean monetarily, but yes, even monetarily, when He deems it. He makes us the head and not the tail; we are above only, not beneath. All this is provided

---

[98] Hebrews 13:5

[99] John 16:33

[100] James 1:2-4 & 12

[101] Romans 5:3-5

[102] 1 Peter 5:8

[103] James 4:7

[104] John 10:10

us *when* we are His true children and we obey the commandments of the Lord our God."[105]

The slow, steady rain coming down added to the dreary
mood inside the warm, cozy farmhouse. Olivia only wrote out
two math problems on her paper, never fully solving the problems for intently listening to their conversation.

Pulling up the quilt over the two cuddled on the couch
Memaw asked Olivia, "Are you cold? Want to join us on the
couch under the blanket?"

Olivia stood and joined them. Memaw spread the quilt to
cover her and placed her hand over Olivia's knees.

"What makes all these promises for us, and not just for when
they were written in Bible times?" asked Stephanie.

"All of God's promises are for us today because the Bible
says we are heirs with Christ.[106] We inherit the right to all
these promises when we accept the sacrifice Jesus made on
Calvary.[107] Because we are the seed of Abraham.[108] Because
God is the same yesterday, today and forever.[109] Because God
changes not."[110]

"When we receive Jesus as our Lord and Savior and keep
the Word of God and live by His Word, we are in right-standing
with Him and place ourselves in a position of being heard when
we pray.[111] Jesus said, '*If anyone loves Me, he will keep My*

---

[105] Deuteronomy 28:1-14

[106] Romans 8:17

[107] 1 Corinthians 12:4

[108] Galatians 3:29

[109] Hebrews 13:8

[110] Psalm 33:11 & Malachi 3:6

[111] John 14:12-15

Word; and My Father will love him, and We will come to him and make Our abode with him. He who does not love Me does not keep My Words; and the Word which you hear is not Mine, but the Father's, who sent Me.'[112] God, the Father Himself, is the One who has stated this fact of the way it will be. If we love Him, we will keep His Word and He will love us and live in us. And He is not a man that He should lie."[113]

"Unfortunately, this is where religion comes in. Many people believe that just because they said a prayer asking Jesus to come into their heart they are saved, period. That they automatically will receive all the blessings God has to offer. That is not exactly what the Bible says anywhere."

Stephanie looked up at Memaw, "I don't understand how that isn't what the Bible says. Isn't that what you quoted just now?"

"Yes, I did say that blessings come when you follow after Christ, but you have to be born again. Salvation is not had by only saying a prayer. And this is where many people get deceived. Not one time in all of Jesus' ministry on Earth did He ever say, "Say this prayer to receive my free gift of salvation."

"But He does say, time and time and time again, that we are to submit to God.[114] Get born again.[115] Put on Christ.[116] Be transformed.[117] Work out our salvation[118]—mind you, I didn't say '*work for*' but '*work out*' our salvation. We couldn't possibly

---

[112] John 14:23&24

[113] Numbers 23:19

[114] James 4:7

[115] John 3:3

[116] Romans 13:14

[117] Romans 12:2

[118] Philippians 2:12

do enough good works to work *for* our salvation. However, we must work out our old selves to put on Christ. We must renew our minds, deny our flesh,[119] and die to our lustful fleshly desires.[120] We must love as He loves.[121] We must be like Christ."[122] All of this is done with Holy Spirit working inside of us. We cannot do it by ourselves, nor for ourselves, without Holy Spirit.

With her brows wrinkled, Stephanie asked, "Then where did we get the Sinner's Prayer?"

"I don't exactly know when, how, or by whom it started, but there are a couple of places in scripture where it states the word, *confession,* as in Romans 10:9 that says, '*...that if you confess with your mouth that Jesus is Lord and believe in your heart that God raised Him from the dead, you will be saved.*'

Memaw reached across Olivia to get Papa's Bible from the end table and turned to the Book of Romans.

"You must continue reading a little below that. It's not merely by confessing alone that saves you, in verse 10 it goes on to explain that, '*...for with the heart a person **believes, resulting in righteousness**, and with the mouth he confesses, resulting in salvation. For the Scripture says, Whoever **believes** in Him will not be disappointed.*' "

"It still doesn't end there, it goes on. But the clencher is even further down after Paul talks about how if people don't believe, how could they call on Him? They need to hear of Him to believe in Him. Preachers were sent, but not everyone

---

[119] Luke 9:23

[120] Galatians 2:20

[121] John 13:34

[122] 1 John 2:6

believed the Good News. He then says, '*So faith comes from hearing, and hearing by the Word of God.*'[123] And there it is."

Stephanie said, "So, if you're not hearing God's Word, you cannot get faith, because hearing God's Word is the only way to get it."

"That's right!" exclaimed Memaw. "Faith is believing God's Word and if you don't believe, you will not result in righteousness."

"But I encouraged Joe to pray to God and ask for healing," with trembling shoulders Stephanie dropped her wet face deeper into Memaw's chest.

"Oh, Sweetheart, you did a good thing in encouraging Joe to go to God."

"I don't know whether Joe has a personal relationship with God or not, and I would encourage him if he doesn't to get one through Jesus and to follow His Word. However, you, being the one who does already have that relationship can definitely pray for Joe to receive God's healing."

She further explained, "That is why we, as Christians, should be serious in our individual walks and following His Word; but also praying for the unsaved people we know. We can stand in the gap and intercede for them when we are in right-standing—we should be doing that."[124]

"Always, when a sinner truly repents and asks for forgiveness and redemption through Jesus Christ, the Lord always hears those who call on Him.[125] '*Let the wicked forsake his way, and the unrighteous man his thoughts; And let him return to the*

---

[123] Romans 10:17

[124] James 5:16

[125] Romans 10:13

Lord, and He will have compassion on him; And to our God, for He will abundantly pardon,' "[126] said Memaw.

"How about this," she suggested, "Let's go to the hospital and talk with and pray for Joe. We can tell him what the Bible says. This way, maybe his mom and dad will surrender their lives as well. We want his entire family knowing Jesus and walking according to His Word."

"Okay," said Stephanie, feeling hope enter in. "I need to wash up, I can't be seen in public like this."

"You go wash up and I'll tell Papa where we're going. Maybe he can come talk with Joe's dad."

Memaw looked at Olivia, "Come on, Sweetie, will you help me grab a few water bottles and fruit bars?"

There was silence in the car as Papa drove to the hospital. The rain continued to fall but it was a soothing, comfortable rain. Memaw and Papa were deep in prayer for the visit with Joe and his parents.

With her finger, Olivia followed the downward path the droplets of water made outside her window.

Mingled thoughts of hope and healing and the possibility of rejection were clouding Stephanie's mind.

"Papa, do you think God will heal Joe if he asks Jesus to save him and heal him?" asked Stephanie.

"I know one thing for sure, God doesn't say 'no' when we ask for salvation. And I believe that God does not want us sick,

---

[126] Isaiah 55:7

He didn't send that sickness upon Joe. But God can use all things for good, and God can use what the enemy intended for evil for the good of people,"[127] answered Papa.

"Does that mean, no?"

"Not at all. God is sovereign, Stephanie. He wants us well and has provided a way for us to be healed. He sent His Son to die a horrible death on a cross so that we could not only be forgiven but healed as well.[128] He determines what He will do with us and our circumstances. Too often, people look at trials and sickness as punishment. God does not punish us that way. The devil is lord of this world.[129] That happened when man gave up the dominion God gave us over things of this Earth. It was passed on to the enemy when Adam and Eve sinned," he explained.

"Yeah," said Stephanie, waiting for the right answer.

"Yes, and when we find we are under a trial or time of tribulation in our life, that was not sent by God, though maybe allowed by God. It is a tough time nevertheless."

"God says in His Word a lot of comforting things when we are going through these times—things like, '*Blessed is the man who remains steadfast under trial, for when he has stood the test he will receive the crown of life, which God has promised to those who love Him.*'"[130]

"And, '*after you have suffered a little while, the God of all grace, who has called you to His eternal glory in Christ, will Himself restore, confirm, strengthen, and establish you.*'"[131]

---

[127] Genesis 50:20

[128] 1 Peter 2:24

[129] 2 Corinthians 4:4

[130] James 1:12

[131] 1 Peter 5:10

"Also, '*Rejoice in hope, be patient in tribulation, be constant in prayer.*' "[132]

Memaw added, "One of my favorites is 2 Corinthians 1:3&4, '*Blessed be the God and Father of our Lord Jesus Christ, the Father of mercies and God of all comfort, who comforts us in all our affliction so that we will be able to comfort those who are in any affliction with the comfort with which we ourselves are comforted by God.*' "

"That sounds like God will heal Joe to me," smiled Stephanie.

Papa laughed. "Yes, most people assume that complete healing and restoration during a trial is the only *right* answer."

"Well, isn't it?" Stephanie felt a bit put out that Papa was encouraging, yet seemed to be backpedaling.

"Honey, you have to understand, that our main job here is to live out the gospel to every person.[133] To live Christ's love in whatever situation we find ourselves in. When we use the good and bad circumstances of life that we walk through to do that, God is glorified."

"No, I'm not saying Joe is gonna die and you should be happy for that. What I am saying is that we all need to realize that sometimes that does happen, and it's not always an unanswered prayer from God."

"To get to live here on earth is not the only right answer. But too often, Christians and non-Christians alike, believe that God did not answer the *right way* when our loved ones die."

"How not? Isn't death the end of it all?" retorted Stephanie.

---

[132] Romans 12:12

[133] Mark 16:15

"Stephanie, when you experienced the beauty of the Supai Falls at the bottom of the Grand Canyon and all its splendor, how did that make you feel?"

The look on Stephanie's face changed as she reminisced on the spectacular memory. "Like I have never seen anything more beautiful in my life; the colors were so rich and vivid, the sound of the water falling was calming, the feel of the mist on my face, refreshing—it was awesome!" she described.

"Can you picture that kind of beauty times 100 at every direction you turn?" asked Papa.

"It's hard to beat that, much less a hundred times over," she said.

"Well Heaven does. The Bible describes it in such a way as being a place where all pain, suffering and tears will not exist.[134] There will be no death, sorrow, nor crying.[135] The devil and any evil of any kind cannot live there."

Papa attempted to describe Heaven, "There is a river that flows right up to God's Throne called the River of Life. You haven't seen crystal clear, clean, sparkling water until you get to see this water. On either side of that River is a tree, the Tree of Life that has 12 crops of fruit on it and twelve times a year it produces fruit."[136]

Papa turned on his windshield wipers and looked left before making his turn.

"You know the feeling of the warm sun shining on your face on a perfect spring day? The glory of God will shine on us day in and day out. There will be no darkness in Heaven.[137] Always,

---

[134] Revelation 21:4

[135] Revelation 20:14

[136] Revelation 22:2

[137] Revelation 22

there will be a glorious light shining upon us everywhere we go, at all times."

"You talked about the beautiful sound the waterfall made, can you just imagine the sound of God speaking to you? The Bible describes it as the sound of rushing water[138] in one text. It also sounds like thunder[139] in another. To many people thunder is a scary sound during storms. From death on, to hear the voice of God like thunder will only be comforting and never scary."

"Heaven isn't called a 'Paradise' for nothing. There will be angels and beasts continually chanting of the holiness of God.[140] Nothing bad or evil at all. Nothing good lacking. Then on the New Earth we live a life, much like we do now, but without hardships, trials, sickness, pain or suffering," said Papa.

"Sounds great, huh?" Without waiting for an answer, he continued, "Heaven will be all that and then some. Best of all, the New Jerusalem will have Jesus, and then eventually God, the Father Himself with us, that we can be with—in the flesh.[141] Can't get any better than that." he smiled, satisfied with his point.

Only silence from the back seat. Stephanie and Olivia sat motionless staring out the side windows, deep in thought over what Papa just described.

"Stephanie, I simply don't agree that staying here is always the only answer to standing in faith and having won the victory over the battle. Heaven isn't a 'second place' answer to our prayers when our request for healing doesn't happen. Going to Heaven doesn't say we 'lose' the battle of faith. Anyone who

---

[138] Revelation 1:15

[139] Revelation 14:2

[140] Revelation 4:8

[141] Revelation 21:3

goes to Heaven wins hugely. We, as Christians, never die," he explained.

"I believe what is most important is not the prayer request, or if it is answered according to what we ask; but instead, **what is done in the name of Christ for the Kingdom** while you are walking through sickness, illness or disease; or trial of any kind."

"The attitude of one walking out their circumstances can minister more to people when they pass on to Heaven if their attitude is one of no fear for going to be with their Lord and Savior. No regrets for being relocated to Heaven over staying here. And no compromise in their stand on faith—even if their end result is death on earth."

Papa was on a roll so he continued, "God's answer to our prayers that we be healed and live here on Earth isn't a win if we've not ministered to someone of God's saving grace, His mercies, and His sacrifice."

"Sometimes more work for the Kingdom can be accomplished through a testimony of no fear of going to Heaven because that isn't a no-to-our-healing answer. Nor is it final death."

"Going to Heaven strong becomes more of an impactful testimony than that of having begged God to stay here on Earth healed; not having received that specific answer, and being afraid of death; sad to go; and questioning why He doesn't answer us by healing us."

"Doing this makes it look like God didn't do His job and leaves many people questioning whether He does still heal, or not. Yes, in fact, God does still heal today."[142]

---

[142] Hebrews 13:8

"His job may have been to have a specific someone reached by us, for their salvation, through this walk we're going through—as He wants all to be saved and to be His children. The real question is, did we do our job?"

"Yeah," said Stephanie, sitting up a little straighter in the back seat and getting fired up. She was feeling more excited to share the Gospel message with Joe.

Memaw chimed in, "Sometimes that can better be accomplished through the platform of having been sick and prayed through. God can use that experience for getting lives saved and encouraging others to live, or die, happily **if** they'd get saved—whether healing comes or not."

"Either way, whether they live through the sickness or die from the sickness, they can be a testimony of unfailing love, no fear, and unequivocal, undying, never-disappointed faith in God. And that ministers more than a quiet miracle of God healing us and allowing us to stay with our loved ones on Earth without anyone ever being told of His grace, mercy and love. Do you see it?" asked Memaw. "Good preaching, Papa," she smiled.

Memaw added, "Even Paul said in his writings to the Philippians that 'according to his expectation and hope, he would not be ashamed in anything, but that with all boldness, he would see to it that Christ would always be exalted in his body, whether by life or by death'."[143]

Papa exclaimed, "Yes! That is precisely what I am trying to say—that is the kind of witness we should be in every trial, even thru sickness unto death. Faith works through love. If we

---

[143] Philippians 1:20

68

have that kind of love and faith, perhaps, and only God knows, but perhaps we'd see and experience more healings."

"That's right," added Memaw, "In the Bible James tells us that we are justified by what we do and not by faith alone."[144]

"Yeah, I get it, almost to the point of asking, 'why would anyone not want to go to Heaven?' " asked Olivia.

"I have often wondered that myself," smiled Papa.

"I would say it's because we want to be with those we love — our family and our friends," added Memaw.

"Yes, I see that. I don't like to be apart from all my family and friends either," agreed Stephanie.

"Then just think about it from God's perspective, neither does He. That is why he wants us all to go be with Him. We are His Creation and He created us to be His family," said Memaw.

Papa put the truck in park and sat silent for a moment offering a prayer in faith that each of his children, and all their families, would continue on a path with Jesus all their lives, as well as all of God's people.

"We're here. Ready to introduce Joe and his family to Jesus?" he asked.

"Let's get in there before we open this Bible and have an all-out Bible study here in the parking lot instead of at Joe's bedside," laughed Memaw.

---

[144] James 2:24

7.

LOVE ALWAYS

"Do you not know that the unrighteous will not inherit the Kingdom of God? Do not be deceived. Neither fornicators, nor idolators, nor adulterers, nor homosexuals, nor sodomites, nor thieves, nor the covetous, nor drunkards, nor revilers, nor extortioners will inherit the Kingdom of God."
1 Corinthians 6:9-10

Memaw wiped her floury hands on her apron to answer the telephone, "Good morning."

"Good morning, Momma, what are you busy with?" asked Laura.

"Olivia's getting her school work done and I'm making tortillas for supper, how about you?"

"I just left the grocery store. I received a call from the school. Apparently, the twins got in trouble so I have to pick them up. I don't have many details other than they were with a group of kids that fought," sighed Laura.

"Oh dear. I'm sure once you get all the details and hear their side of it, it won't be as bad as it sounds," with a whisper, "I hope."

"Yeah, well, for their sakes' I hope you're right," said Laura.

"Momma, Mark has a chiropractor appointment. Can I please drop the twins off to you until Ethan is off work? He's loading a truck. As soon as he's done, he can head home to have this family discussion."

"What's wrong with my little guy that he needs to see the chiropractor?" asked Memaw, "Yes, definitely, bring the twins by."

"Oh, he's colicky, nothing serious. I've got to get driving—it's getting warm for him in the car seat, he needs the air running. Thanks Mom!"

"You bet, drive safe, Honey. See you soon."

Memaw began praying for her grandchildren as she rolled out the next tortilla. "Oh twins. Lord, thank You that You are an ever-present help in times of trouble."

Memaw was ironing the collar of Papa James' shirt and Olivia was dusting the living room when Raelene walked in with Laura, carrying Mark.

"Hi Momma, Hi Olivia." greeted Laura with an upset tone. She hugged and kissed each one on the cheek.

"Awww, how's my baby?" asked Memaw, reaching for Baby Mark.

"Fussy." answered Laura, happily handing him off.

"Hi Memaw," said Raelene, going in for a hug. "Hi Olivia."

"Hi Sweetheart." Memaw gave a tight side hug for having Mark in her arms, and kissed her cheek. She held on to show love and support in her time of trouble. "Where's Reuben?"

"He's coming. Momma asked him to bring in your mail."

"Would you like a snack and drink? I made Papa horchata last night, you'll find it in the white gallon pitcher. The glass jar is sweet tea," offered Memaw.

"Thank you," said Raelene walking away solemnly.

Laura told what little she knew, "I don't even know where to begin, Momma. Apparently, some of the boys on the football team started making fun of a gay boy in the cafeteria. The teasing turned into shoving him around and soon an all-out beating," she sighed holding back tears.

"The fight was broken up and only some of the football players were taken to the principal's office. The young man was walked to the nurse. When Principal Howard learned that not all the kids involved were in his office, he sent for the rest. They were gathered at a lunchroom table celebrating. Because the Vice Principal didn't know who had been involved, he took everyone sitting at the table—including the twins."

Hoping the twins weren't actually celebrating the fight, Memaw asked with reservation, "Please tell me Reuben didn't participate in beating that young man. But why were they sent home? And Raelene? What did she have to do with it?"

"Good questions. That is what we'll have to find out once Ethan gets home and we have this discussion," said Laura, reaching for a tissue from the end table. "I have to get Mark over to Dr. Paulson for his appointment. We'll be back." Laura lifted Baby Mark out of Memaw's arms and headed out.

Memaw sat silently in prayer for her grandchildren and all involved, especially the gay young man. She was interrupted by Reuben walking in with her mail.

"Hi Memaw. Here's your mail," said Reuben dropping it on the table in the foyer. He hugged and kissed Memaw.

Olivia blushed when Reuben walked in. "Hi Reuben."

"Hi Olivia," he barely looked at her but did give her a side hug.

Memaw said, "Raelene has set out a snack and drinks in the kitchen, let's join her."

"Yes Ma'am," was all he said and followed.

Awkward silence filled the room. Olivia admired Raelene and always enjoyed talking with her, but today was different. She thought it best to keep her distance and talk to a minimum. Hearts were full of obvious remorse and hopefully regret.

Memaw wasn't going to ask for details, especially if their mother and father hadn't yet had their discussion with the twins. She would wait to be told what would be shared with her, if anything at all.

"Do you have any homework to get done? Maybe you oughta get that done and out of the way?" she suggested.

"Yes Ma'am," answered Raelene reaching for her backpack at the foot of the stool she was on. Opening it up she pulled out books and her notebook and set them unopened on the island counter in front of her.

Reuben sat silent staring at his glass of horchata and only picking at pieces of the rolled tortilla in front of him.

"I'm starting a salad for supper," said Memaw, turning on the radio. She turned the volume down just to where sound could break up the awkward silence.

She pulled out vegetables. In a low whisper, she sang along with the song playing.

"Is Papa here? Can I go talk with him?" asked Reuben.

"Mijo, he's at Mr. Larson's helping him put in a transmission, I'm sorry," responded Memaw.

"I can't concentrate enough to get any school work done." said Raelene, a tear rolling down her cheek.

"I can imagine you're upset, twins, I'm sorry. Why don't you two talk it out on the porch. It'll make you feel better," she encouraged.

Neither one moved.

"I'm so angry." said Reuben, breaking the silence. "I know what we did is wrong, but what he's doing is wrong, too. No one deserves to be beat, but it's so hard to stand up to a big majority."

"Why didn't I stop them? But a part of me wanted this kid to knock it off and maybe this would beat into him, that what he's doing is wrong. I felt so helpless but hate seeing what he's bringing to our school's reputation. We are a Christian high school — he should know better. Why do Christians have to conform? What message would I have given if I would have tried to stop them? Then I would have been accused of being gay. Maybe even with him." Reuben rattled out his frustration.

Reuben was a tough kid who didn't shed a tear. Being troubled with regret, confusion and anger, he was red-eyed and red-faced.

Raelene, on the other hand, had a steady stream of tears. She no longer held back the sobbing sounds that came with every breath. Olivia handed her the box of tissues and gave a side hide. Memaw walked around the island to hug them all.

After taking a deep breath, while hugging the twins she began, "Heavenly Father, we praise You in all things. Thank You at all times. And love You always. You are worthy to be praised and worshiped, even in the hard things — especially in the hard things. Help the hurting hearts of all the children involved. I pray that each and every one of them would have someone to hold them and love them through the emotions they are feeling, and to answer the questions they have. I pray for this young man who is hurting inside, as much as outside, that he would physically be alright and not have any lasting injuries from the beating; and that his heart would come to heal and be restored back to You. Back to feeling loved, as well as being able to love others in a healthy manner for his good and Your glory. In Jesus' name we pray. Amen."

The four huddled in a hug with no sound other than Raelene's crying.

"I know your parents will have answers for you. They can help you sort through all the emotions you're feeling right now. What you did, or didn't do—as the case may be—you will have consequences for, you know that, right? But healing will come. And love is always behind every discipline, remember that," encouraged Memaw.

It was not her place to have corrected the twins or to discipline them for their shared part in the unfortunate incident.

She tried to console her grandchildren without condoning what they had participated in, "I don't know all the details to have much to say. And that's not for me to know before you tell your parents. But I can say, I certainly hope you two don't ever think that God can't, or won't, forgive you for your part in this, or this young man for what he is choosing to do. God will forgive him and you both; it is important you go to Him and ask Him to. I will pray that this young man will reach a point in his life that he, too, will go to God and ask for forgiveness and change his ways."

"While I know you're upset with this kid's choices, and I understand being upset over his decision to sin, you cannot hate the sinner, or condemn the sinner. That is not your place."

"God is love. You cannot say you love God while you hate your brother. Hate will not heal. Hate will not discipline. Hate will not even help you feel better. Hate accomplishes nothing. Only love does."

Memaw continued, "You have to understand that God loves this precious people. He loves them as much as He loves you and me and the people He has called to preach. They are just as special to Him as well. Homosexuals and others that make up all those initials are sinning at this moment, the same way I sin when I get caught up in gossip. The same way you sin when you lie to get out of trouble. The only difference being, when we sin, we immediately repent and work at not sinning again."

"We have to pray that they come to see that they have believed a lie from Satan."

"Pray that they learn the truth that they were not born this way."

"Pray that they realize they are making a choice to behave in a manner that does displease the Lord."

"Pray that they learn they're choosing an unhealthy way of life for their bodies and mental states. That they are regrooving their brains, literally altering them to believe they accept something that is bad for them."

"And pray that they know that God loves them and wants them to repent and that they'd ask Holy Spirit to help them not sin. He can and will forgive them and help them all, if they will go to Him and ask for it."

"God calls us to love both our neighbor but especially those who are our enemies.[145] I'm not saying he is your enemy, but the point I'm trying to make is that if we are called to love both

---

[145] Matthew 5:43-44

ends of the spectrum from those close to us as our neighbors and family, to the other end of that spectrum—our enemies—how much more so everybody in between those two ends?" said Memaw.

"Additionally, as I make every effort to get through to you that you must first love, I also want to get through the point that you cannot condone or participate with sin. We are to lovingly and prayerfully confront, alone first, our brother or sister in Christ with what sin we know they are outwardly doing before we go to them with a crowd.[146] Nor are we responsible for making them pay for their sin. The Bible is very specific about how to handle the sin our brothers or sisters in Christ are involved in. Read it in Matthew 18:15-17."

The twins' questions went deeper. "I know, Memaw, that's why I feel so guilty over how neither of us stopped the ones hitting him. But deep inside, we kind of wanted him to stop giving us a bad name," cried Raelene. "I feel terrible for feeling that way," she sobbed.

"I understand, Rae, guilt is painful. That is why the sooner you take care of confessing these feelings to God and understanding them and how to handle them, you don't have to live with the guilt. But it is important you learn from this and don't place yourself in this situation again. Let me ask you two this, was it you who encouraged the beating?"

"No." said the twins at the same time.

"Did you participate in hitting him?"

"No!" they exclaimed.

"Would you have been able to stop the others from beating him?" was the final question.

---

[146] Matthew 18:15

Raelene said, "No."

Reuben, on the other hand, remained silent and head down.

"Reuben?" questioned Memaw with raised eyebrow.

"You know, being one of the guys that is looked up to on the team, I keep asking myself that same question. That's where the deep sense of guilt comes from. I think I might have been able to stop them. I also feel sick to my stomach because I don't think I wanted to make them stop. Not until it got ugly and they weren't letting up on him. Then I tried to make them stop but by then, it was too late. There were too many kicking at him and they were beyond hearing me or even feeling me pull them off of him," admitted Reuben with tearing eyes for the first time.

"Oh Reuben," sighed Memaw heavy-hearted. She walked back over to their side of the island again.

"Yeah. That's gotta hurt," she said placing a hand on his hot shoulder. She could feel the heat through his shirt as he held his breath. His face and neck red for trying not to allow the cry to escape.

"Honey. I understand your predicament. But not stopping someone from committing a wrong you are present for, when you could have, is just like participating with the wrong your-self. You understand that, right?"

Memaw was hoping that the facts would show her grand-children were innocent and being wrongly accused. That was not appearing to be the case. Even if the twins could prove they never laid a hand on the young man, they also didn't stop it from happening when they could have.

"I'm sorry, Memaw." cried Reuben. All 173 pounds of muscle and strength collapsed into Memaw's arms as he let it all out.

Through his sobs, Reuben asked, "Why? Why would he choose to do such a stupid thing? He knows it is a sin to be gay."[147]

"Mijo, I can't answer that for him. I don't know anything about him. But you need to pray for him. Unfortunately, too often, some people hurt inside so they do things outwardly to either hurt others or themselves."

Not waiting for an answer, she continued, "People choose to be homosexual for various reasons, some can't even explain it. Unfortunately, it could be because they were molested as a child or had been raped. Maybe they were influenced by someone close to them. Perhaps they've been rejected so often by either people of the opposite sex or their own family that they're looking for love from someone — anyone that will give it, even if it is in a sinful way."

"It could be because so many are choosing this lifestyle to be hip and they follow the fad it seems to have become — as dangerous a trend as it is. No one but God truly knows. But most importantly, no one but God can truly judge them for it."

"The Bible says it is a sin, right, Memaw?" asked Raelene.

"Yes, Baby, it does. Throughout the Old Testament and the New Testament. However, we are to despise the sin, not the sinner. Christians need to respond to sinners with grace and truth and love," said Memaw.

Olivia began to pace and looked very uncomfortable. Memaw noticed but didn't address it.

Reuben asked, "But Memaw, what could we have done?"

"What did Jesus do? Did he not stand up for the woman who was about to be stoned because she was found committing adultery with a married man? He wrote on the ground and asked,

---

[147] Leviticus 18:22

'*Let him who is without sin among you be the first to throw a stone at her.*'[148] Then, He proceeded to write something more on the ground. The Bible never says what He wrote. But, think about it, when everyone walked away, He turned to her and asked, '*who is still here condemning you?*' She answered '*No one, Lord.*' He said, '*Neither do I condemn you; go, and from now on **sin no more**.*' "[149]

"Yeah, but I'm not Jesus to call anyone out on their sin, nor forgive anyone of their sin," said Reuben.

"That's not the part you could have done. What part could have you done?"

"I know. And that's what's eating me up inside," said Reuben solemnly. "Because I truly know what I could have done and should have done. And I didn't."

Reuben's remorse was obvious. Memaw felt heartache over the entire situation, for all involved.

"Okay, that's now in the past. What could you do now? Beyond whatever your parents ask you to as your discipline. What could you do to help someone who claims to be homosexual from now on, or for this same young fellow, even?" asked Memaw.

"I guess find out where the Bible says homosexuality is a sin and confront them with it?" answered Rae.

"Perhaps, but there is so much more to that. What are you going to tell someone who tells you they didn't choose to be that way, that they were born homosexual?"

Raelene just opened her eyes wide, not knowing the answer and feeling overwhelmed. It's not easy.

---

[148] John 8:1-7

[149] John 8:8-11

"Yeah, there's a lot of praying and studying and asking God to guide and direct you to His Word about His revelations on the matter. A lot of people do believe they were born that way," said Memaw.

"Were they?" asked Reuben.

"No. God created us and designed sexual relationships to be between one woman and one man.[150] He even makes sure to say it is not to be done outside of the marriage bond of that one man and one woman.[151] He created Adam a man, and Eve as a woman. He created their bodies to fit when brought together," she began to explain.

"Oh, this is getting weird," stood Reuben taking steps back as if to back away from the conversation. "Not cool sitting here listening to my grandmother tell me of the birds and the bees."

They all laughed over Reuben's discomfort on the topic.

"It isn't dirty, nasty or wrong, Reuben. People have made it appear to be those things because of how Satan has corrupted the view of it all, and how this world we live in has been distorted to believe it is not as beautiful an act, or as lovely a gift from God, Himself."

"Stooop!" said Reuben.

"Okay. I'll change the way I talk about it. I'm sorry, Reuben. But truly, you have to be mature enough to hear it, in order to understand it as God intends it to be, and be able to share," said Memaw.

"I'm not so sure I want to be the one sharing these truths," said Reuben. "How about I set up an appointment for all them to come to you and you share these truths?" They laughed.

---

[150] Genesis 2:24

[151] Mark 10:6-12

It was hard to stay on topic and discuss this serious behavior when the kids were feeling so uncomfortable about the topic. Memaw had to think fast and talk in terms they would hear.

Fortunately for Memaw, Papa walked in as they were laughing. "Hey, my twins are here. But aren't you supposed to be in school?" He glanced at the clock on the wall, walking over to get his hugs in. Then to Memaw to kiss her cheek. He smiled his greeting to Olivia.

Reuben and Raelene filled him in on the details of their day. Memaw poured Papa a glass of iced tea and made him a quesadilla.

"So, to put behind us what we cannot change now," said Memaw, "I asked them to think of ways they could stop that from happening again. Rae said to confront them with what the Bible says about it. We're discussing all the things the Bible does have to say about the topic."

"And it is making Reuben *very* uncomfortable," said Raelene laughing. The whole room laughed.

"Yeah, getting the birds and the bees lesson from Memaw isn't easy to sit through," said Reuben.

"Well, the Bible does say we are to confront, not condemn, but confront our fellow brothers and sisters with gentle correction in love when they are sinning.[152] Without going into detail, I will say that the devil has a counterfeit for a lot of good things God created. While God created sex to be healthy, normal and beautiful, Satan has distorted it in our mind's eye and made it to be dirty, unnatural and even unhealthy. Homosexuality is only one of the means for which he uses to do that. He also

---

[152] Galatians 6:1

83

uses pornography, bad language, promiscuity, adultery, incest, bestiality, polygamy, prostitution, rape, molestation..."

Reuben interrupted Papa, "I thought it was going to get easier to hear from you *not* giving details?" he sank down into his stool.

Everyone laughed. Olivia walked out from under the doorway from the laundry room and sat on a stool beside Raelene.

"It's not an easy topic, son. Maybe this world is in the predicament we're in because sexuality is a difficult topic and easier to ignore and not talk about, than to sit here and listen when it is covered," said Papa.

"It is imperative that sexuality be taught correctly, otherwise you learn it from the world's view, accepting homosexuality as natural. It is most definitely not natural."

"Even homosexuals have to convince themselves it is okay and feels right; if they're honest with themselves they'll admit it isn't. Most don't want to be honest with themselves."

"Why do you think so many homosexuals are not happy with their lives. They pretend to be. They have to justify their lifestyle. But true happiness, by definition of the word, they are not. The suicide rate among homosexuals is too high to prove me wrong. Look up the statistics," said Papa passionately.

"The Bible has a lot to say about it. When He speaks of 'sodomy' it refers to a man having sexual relations with another man, which is another word for describing the sin of homosexuality."

Papa walked into the adjoining room to get a dictionary.

"I'll have to look up this word. Here it is, according to Webster's Dictionary, the word 'licentiousness' refers to one who "disregards accepted rules and standards, one who is morally unrestrained, especially in sexual matters," he read.

The room remained silent and suddenly felt the seriousness of the reality of the topic. Papa continued, "When the Pharisees questioned Jesus about divorce, He answered them everything that needed to be said on the subject of sexual ethics. He said, *'Have you not read that He who created them from the beginning made them male and female, and said, Therefore a man shall leave his father and mother and hold fast to his wife, and the two shall become one flesh? So they are no longer two, but one flesh. What God has joined together, let no man separate.'*[153]

"Jesus very specifically addressed that God created male and female and that the man is to take on a wife and those two shall become one flesh. God went so far as to commission man and woman to 'be fruitful and multiply.'[154] That not only means have babies. It means to make more Christ-like ones. You see, we are supposed to be equally yoked with another believer and make babies to become more Christ-like ones," said Papa.

"As a matter of fact, the only option Jesus ever mentioned, other than marriage, was celibacy.[155] That's when you stay single and never get married nor have relations, you instead vow to give your life to God."

"That's right, now that you say it." said Memaw. "I'd never really ever thought about that."

"Why then, would people choose to be gay?" asked Reuben.

"Like Memaw said," said Raelene, "Because of molestation or rape, influences or rejection. Or just following fads—so many are claiming to be these days, because it's popular to be gay."

---

[153] Mark 10:7-9

[154] Genesis 1:27-28

[155] 1 Corinthians 7:7-9

"Sadly, I think Raelene is right. In today's times, many of the occasions are a way of standing out as going against the grain, or as you guys would call it, 'going rogue' or 'being a rebel' because being different is often looked at as being cool," said Memaw.

"Unfortunately, it is also an evil presence that comes upon some who suffer from an intimacy and identity disorder. Satan lies to them about why they feel the way they do about themselves and they believe his deceptive lies," added Papa.

"God tells us He is close to the broken-hearted, those who are confused, or hurting, or tempted.[156] If we, when under pressure or feeling oppressed, or under bad circumstances, or tempted would go to God, we could resist those temptations. He clearly addresses it in His Word when He says, '*No temptation has overcome you but such as is common to man; and God is faithful, who will not allow you to be tempted beyond what you are able, but with the temptation will provide the way of escape also, so that you will be able to endure it.*' "[157]

Papa continued, "God knows these temptations come upon us. When lustful thoughts come, we should go to God for help and He provides a way for us to escape them."

Memaw added, "But if we don't believe that He can and will; or, we choose to ignore Him, our choices become sin because we outright follow through with the lustful thoughts."

"When we feel ourselves being influenced to engage in sinful behavior—any one of the many types of sin—we should go to God for help. Period. He is always a present help in times of trouble."[158]

---

[156] Psalm 34:18

[157] 1 Corinthians 10:13

[158] Psalm 46:1

"We must have the strength to say 'no' and choose to do right. Easy, it is not; but neither is it impossible. And He provides the help," said Papa.

"Unfortunately, the less you go to God for help and cave to the temptation, the easier the sin becomes to the point of eventually no longer appearing to be evil and thinking it is good and acceptable. It becomes 'iniquity'. Iniquity is when we not only sin, but we willfully sin and even find delight in sin," said Memaw.

"Yes, but the Bible covers that too. It says, '*Woe to those who call evil good, and good evil; who substitute darkness for light and light for darkness...*' " [159] said Papa.

He added, "There is always hope for the sinner. Homosexuals do come out of homosexuality; and sinners of any kind of sexual sin, be it lust, adulterers, pornographers, fornicators, even molesters and rapists. God loves us all so much that He is always willing to hear the sinner's cry of repentance."

"We sin and He forgives us. It is no different for those who are sinning sexually. God, will, hear, them, too."

"God often gets through to these people using other Christians who have the love enough to share truth gently and with authentic humility."

"We also have Holy Spirit's help. Holy Spirit restores wholeness," added Memaw.

"Though most times, we have to earn the right to speak into their lives," she said, "we can't just confront them and share what the Bible says about their choices and expect they will be motivated to change immediately. Not everyone is ready to hear and repent instantly. It's important that we let love and

---

[159] Isaiah 5:20

compassion be our motive, not hatred or repulsion. But most importantly, make them see that they are sinning against God and that leads to their destruction in Hell."

In perfect time, Ethan walked in the side door. Greetings were exchanged and Memaw, Papa and Olivia cleared the room. Ethan asked the children to sit in the living room, when Laura walked in.

Laura said, "Mark's with Memaw on the front porch."

Standing up and greeting his wife with a kiss, Ethan said, "Good, let's start in prayer."

Papa walked to his shop. Memaw, Mark and Olivia sat on the front porch.

"Memaw, I heard what you said in there. What happens when a girl is not gay but another girl touches her wrong. Is God mad at the girl who is not gay. Will she go to Hell?"

Tears welled in Memaw's eyes, "Oh Sweetheart. God is not mad at the girl who got touched. He is sad and hurting that someone would have touched an innocent girl that way. He talks about not hurting children in the Bible. People who do, are in a lot of trouble with Him. The children aren't in trouble, no." she hugged Olivia.

"May I ask, who it is that got touched? Was it you, Olivia?"

Olivia played with Mark's shoelace and brushed away a tear.

"I only ask so that we can pray to God and ask Him to help the girl it happened to. And in case it was you, to say I will do all I can so that doesn't ever happen to you again."

"What about when I leave, how can you protect me after I'm gone?"

"Mija, what makes you think you're leaving?"

"I always go back."

"Honey, we have no intention of sending you back. You're with us until you're eighteen unless you don't want to be here. If you want, you can stay until you go off to school, or get married, or you get a place of your own."

Olivia had to be certain so asked, "Are you sure?"

"How many homes have you lived in?" Memaw had to ask.

"I don't know. I don't remember."

This poor child.

"Why do you want me here?" asked Olivia.

"Because we love you. Because Jesus loves you. Because you are important to Jesus and to Papa and I, and to our entire family. Because you are special. Because you are worth it. Because you are fun. Because you are beautiful. Because you are chosen. Should I keep going?"

"No one has ever said any of those things about me before."

"I'm sorry for that. You are all that and so much more. You should have been hearing that all your life. I can't help what happened to you, or what wasn't done for you in the past. But I can tell you beginning today. You are all those things and so much more. You are smart. You are strong. You are an overcomer."

Instead of smiling Olivia cried. She cried like she had never cried before. She fell limp in Memaw's arms and cried her little heart out.

Memaw held her and cried with her thanking her Heavenly Father that not a single tear was being wasted. Because He was bottling up each and every one.[160]

"Thank You Heavenly Father for Your love for this precious child. Thank You for sending Olivia into our lives, we are

---

[160] Psalm 56:8

richer for it. May her heart heal and be healthy and strong with love for You and for others. I pray, in Jesus' name, that Olivia would forgive all the people in her past that have hurt her and touched her in wrong and mean and inappropriate ways. Please heal her physically and heal her spirit, Lord. Thank You. We love You. Amen.

8.

UNTIL WE MEET AGAIN

"Enter by the narrow gate; for wide is the gate and broad is the way that leads to destruction, and there are many who go in by it. Because narrow is the gate and difficult is the way which leads to life, and there are few who find it."
Matthew 7:13 & 14

*I*t's hard for Olivia to believe she has a home. The smell of food warming in the oven brings comfort knowing she will be fed today. What a good feeling to have a family to gather with often for entertaining, adventures, even work. They do most everything together. Today was a difficult day. They would need each other's support and prayers.

The family was getting back to Memaw and Papa's house after a funeral service. All were grieving and heavy-hearted over the loss of one so young and such a precious child of God. Tyler and Susie's families met when they were three years old as neighbors on the same country road. At sixteen years old Tyler had been in a tragic accident and died an untimely death. His love and dedication for Christ, even at such a young age, left an impression on all who knew him. While the family grieved over the thought of Tyler being gone from this Earth, they also rejoiced over the fact that he was now with Jesus Christ.

The ladies were putting out drinks and setting the tables. Some of the children ran outside to play, others milled around the living room. The men were on the front porch visiting and watching over the youngest babies.

Having grown up as friends the same age, Susie was closest to Tyler and having the hardest time with his passing. She sat alone in the family room tucked under a blanket as though wanting to hide. Memaw and Olivia went in, sat beside her and hugged Susie, not letting go.

In a croaky voice from crying Susie whispered, "For sure and for certain Tyler is with Jesus, right?"

"Ultimately, Jesus is the only one who knows that with certainty as God declared Him the Judge of all.[161] We must be certain to ask Jesus to be Lord of our lives and Holy Spirit to transform us.[162] We must produce good fruit as a result.[163] We know Tyler asked Jesus to be Lord of his life, we were there when he went forward at church when he was younger. It was also evident in his day-to-day living that he did glorify God. His life's choices were according to what Jesus taught we should live, even at his young age. God knows the heart to determine if someone is truly a disciple of Christ. He even records all we do and say in books to judge us by our life's actions when we approach His Throne, as we all will.[164] No one can get to Heaven by alone doing good deeds, no matter how

---

[161] John 5:22

[162] John 3:3

[163] Matthew 7:16-20

[164] Revelation 20:12

intentional their heart is to being good.[165] Doing good things does not save us,[166] that is clear in the Bible. However, good works should follow our salvation.[167] That, too, is clear in the Bible," said Memaw.

After a brief silence she continued, "Oh but, there are two small words in the Bible that, at first, seem to be insignificant, but they actually shake me up!"

"What two words?" asked Susie.

"Few and many."

"Few and many," repeated Susie. "Where in the Bible are those two words used together?"

Reaching for Papa's Bible from the end table, Memaw read aloud from Matthew chapter 7 and began in verse 13, " *'Enter through the narrow gate; for the gate is wide and the way is broad that leads to destruction, and there are **many** who enter through it. For the gate is small and the way is narrow that leads to life, and there are **few** who find it.'* What do you take away from that?"

"I thought that if you believe in your heart and say with your mouth that Jesus is Lord, you are saved?" asked Susie.

"That is how you initiate the invitation to invite Jesus in to your life to save you. But whether you truly do believe in your heart, or not, is only known by you and God. When one truly means it and undoubtedly gets saved there is a transformation that happens inside because Holy Spirit comes to live in you. You then desire to do good things that glorify God and stay away from bad choices. The Bible speaks of you becoming a

---

[165] Ephesians 2:8&9

[166] Romans 3:23-28

[167] James 2:17&18

new creature in Christ because the old nature is passed away and there is a newness that comes within you.[168] To become new means you no longer desire to do the bad things that the old you used to do, and you have an innate desire to do Godly things because you realize how sin separates you from God." paused Memaw.

"Let's read on right from where we left off when the Bible spoke of the way being narrow that leads to life, and there are few who find it. It continues on to say, *'Beware of the false prophets, who come to you in sheep's clothing, but inwardly are ravenous wolves. You will know them by their fruits. Grapes are not gathered from thorn bushes nor figs from thistles, are they? So every good tree bears good fruit, but the bad tree bears bad fruit. A good tree cannot produce bad fruit, nor can a bad tree produce good fruit. Every tree that does not bear good fruit is cut down and thrown into the fire. So then, you will know them by their fruits. Not everyone who says to Me, Lord, Lord, will enter the Kingdom of Heaven, but he who does the will of My Father who is in Heaven will enter. Many will say to Me on that day, Lord, Lord, did we not prophecy in Your name, and in Your name cast out demons, and in Your name perform many miracles? And then I will declare to them, Depart from Me, I never knew you.'* "[169]*

Memaw allowed that to sink in. We can say anything, but the real question is, are we living out what we are saying? Always—not just in front of people. Are our actions true and honorable even when no one is watching? God truly knows all

---

[168] 2 Corinthians 5:17

[169] Matthew 7:15-23

that—He knows all things. He knows the intentions of our heart and why we do things."

"That's enough to scare the tar out of anyone," said Susie.

"It shouldn't be when you know you're doing things solely because it is glorifying to God. This is why we should reverence God and live as He describes in His Word when Jesus becomes Lord of our lives. Then we're certain we'll be one of the few," Memaw said.

"A very good example that proves God knows the heart of a person is found with the Pharisee in the Bible. The Pharisees got a bad rap as being hypocrites because they were legalistic. Truly, they were well-educated, well-versed in the Torah, which is the first five books of the Old Testament, and they followed the Law religiously."

"In Greek, the definition of a Pharisee is *one who separates himself, or keeps away from impure persons or things in order to reach the degree of holiness and righteousness required to get close with God.* The Pharisees observed every Levitical Law of purity. They did not associate themselves with any person that wasn't strictly following the Law. They paid their tithes. They were zealous for God and His ways. They memorized the first five books of the Old Testament."

Susie looked at Memaw and said, "They sound like strong Christians."

"And yet, Jesus called the Pharisees 'offspring of vipers.'[170] They were also called 'whited tombs which outwardly appear beautiful, but inwardly are full of dead men's bones,'[171] 'blind

---

[170] Matthew 12:34

[171] Matthew 23:27

95

guides who strain out a gnat and swallow a camel.'[172] All that means that they take care to look holy outwardly and do nothing that would appear to be wrong. But inside, they are ugly and making choices for wrong reasons—to look like they're good, holy and righteous in the eyes of people."

Looking down Susie only whispered, "Wow."

"But God doesn't want people to behave religiously. To do right things for the wrong reasons, or with the wrong heart. And God will know."

"He wants a sincere relationship with us. The only way to get that is to learn what He says in the Bible by reading it and hearing it preached and explained. As we learn His Word, we must believe it and live it out. *Believing* being the key word. When you believe a certain thing, you live it out. But to know what you believe you have to learn about it."

In walked Reuben and Raelene with Matthew and Stephanie following behind. "Can we come in?" asked Reuben.

Memaw looked at Susie. She smiled at her cousins and patted the couch inviting them to sit beside her.

Memaw filled them in, "We're talking about whether one is truly saved or not. About how Pharisees from the Bible took great care to do all the right things according to the Law. They appeared to be holy and righteous in all things on the outside, but inwardly, their reasons for doing it was actually to bring glory to themselves, for accolades and credit for being so holy."

She reiterated, "When you trust Jesus to be Lord of your life and believe what the Bible says, you live it out. When you give God complete control over you, is when you are truly saved. Otherwise, you are just 'talking the talk and not walking

---

[172] Matthew 23:24

the walk' and that gets to be dangerous ground to tread. The Bible says, that unless our righteousness exceeds the righteousness of the Pharisees, we will by no means enter the Kingdom of Heaven.' "[173]

The Bible still lay open on Memaw's lap. Susie read the verse in Matthew that talked about the broad road that many will enter and the narrow road that few will enter.

Olivia was getting more and more comfortable talking with the family. She said, "You have said this same thing in different ways. With Annette on our walk, and on our drive home from taking Matthew to his friend's house."

"That's because the same truths are written out in different ways throughout the New Testament of the Bible," said Memaw.

"How can we be certain we are living out what the Bible says?" asked Stephanie.

"It's impossible, on your own merit, to be good enough to get into Heaven. No one can get in by alone doing what, to us, are all right things. For all have sinned and fall short of the glory of God.[174] All the right things are only right to **you**, according to **your** own opinion, based on what **your** standard of 'right' is. And what is right for you, or even asked of you by God isn't exactly what is right for, or even asked of one by God, for another, much less everyone." answered Memaw.

"Wait, I'm confused," said Matthew. "Doesn't God expect us all to follow His Word the same way—the right way? Why would He ask some of us to do His Word, and not others?"

"Good question, Matthew. Yes, he expects us all to follow His Word, however, once you are close enough to God to 'hear'

---

[173] Matthew 5:20

[174] Romans 3:23

Him speak to you through His Word when you're reading it, through other people, or by Holy Spirit to convict your heart of something, that conviction is strictly for you. He didn't make us using a cookie cutter. As well as looking differently, we think differently, act and react to situations differently, and struggle with different sins."

Sitting up closer to the edge of the sofa Memaw made her next point, "God calls some of us to refrain from things that others are allowed to do. For instance, not everyone struggles with gossip. Some people are able to walk away from a group that begins to gossip, while some people get caught up in the gossip and desire to be there to hear more of it and participate in it by sharing it. Some girls can wear makeup without obsessing over themselves and their looks, while others get self-absorbed over their looks and what they look like with or without it with pride. Same thing with guys over their muscular bodies. And several other examples."

"When you are close enough to the Lord to really hear his voice—which isn't usually audible, although He has and can as He can do anything, He relays messages to us through Holy Spirit when we feel in our hearts that what we're doing is wrong. Whether we choose to follow His leading or not is up to us; He will never force us to. God can use people to relay messages to us. While we read His Word, He relays messages to us. While we pray to Him and sit quietly and open our hearts to listen to what He has to say to us. He gives some visions, others dreams.[175] There are many ways God speaks to us," explained Memaw.

---

[175] Acts 2:17

"Sometimes I wish He would speak audibly so that I know I'm sure to pick the right choice every time," said Reuben.

"I wish He would force me to make the right choice," said Olivia.

Memaw looked at Olivia and explained to her, "To force someone into doing something is not real, true, genuine love."

"That's why it's so important to be close to Him so that you know when it's Him speaking to you and leading you." said Matthew with excitement for understanding.

"Exactly!" responded Memaw with equal excitement that he was getting it. "But back to your original question, so because some of us have struggles that others' don't necessarily need to be corrected from, God asks some of us not to wear makeup. Or not to work out for muscle building. Or not to eat certain foods, or drink certain drinks, or speak certain words, or participate with certain activities. It all depends on whether you do it for self, or for His glory, as all things we do and say should be to glorify God only. Make sense?"

"Total sense," answered Matthew.

Reuben punched Matthew's arm, "So don't go getting cocky, Superman." They all laughed.

"Along the lines of what Susie read to you, many will call Him Lord, and say they truly do believe in Jesus and love Him and read the Bible. But unless you actually, physically and verbally and heartily make the actions of confessing with your mouth Jesus as Lord, and believing in your heart that God raised Him from the dead, will you be saved. The Bible says, *'for with the heart a person believes, resulting in righteousness, and with the mouth he confesses, resulting in salvation.'*[176] It

---

[176] Romans 10:10

takes genuine faith to do that, not half a thought or just speaking meaningless words. Faith only comes from hearing, and hearing by the Word of God."[177] said Memaw.

"Sadly, and too often, we only think of the half of that verse and consider ourselves sealed. Many disregard the *resulting in righteousness* part. Many only say, 'believe in your heart and confess with your mouth and you will be saved'. That isn't all that verse says."

"Yes, and when it is a genuine conversion, change toward being and doing good comes with it and you become judged by your fruit. Just like I read, good fruit comes from a good tree; and bad fruit comes from bad trees,"[178] added Susie.

"That's right," agreed Memaw.

"Pray for Joe and his family, guys, they refused to receive Jesus as their Savior when Papa offered to pray with them at the hospital. They believe they're already saved because they love Jesus so much and go to church when they can and are generally good people and don't do things that hurt others," said Stephanie with a sad countenance.

She continued sharing, "But when Papa asked about what in their lives changed after surrendering to Jesus, they didn't know what he meant. They answered that they have always loved Jesus. They have always done good. They have always tried hard to make some time to read their Bible and go to Church. They weren't able to read it every day, or go to church every week, but who does? 'Life is busy', they said."

"Sorry, Steph," said Raelene hugging her cousin sympathetically. "We'll definitely pray."

---

[177] Romans 10:17

[178] Matthew 7:17&18

"Sadly, there are many who believe that way," said Memaw. "Even Christians who have made a profession of faith and do attend church weekly are not making a concerted effort to live out and walk the way of the Word daily, attempting to glorify God in all that is said and done. They grow complacent. They get what is often called, 'cold'. The Bible describes it and speaks of that in the book of Revelation."

She turned to the third chapter of Revelation and explained that, "Jesus had a message he gave to seven Churches, and to the Church of Laodicea he said, *'I know your deeds, that you are neither cold or hot; I wish you were cold or hot. Because you are lukewarm, and neither hot or cold, I will spit you out of My mouth.'* "[179]

Memaw paused to make the next point very clear, "It is very important that you know that **God does not reject people and send them to Hell**. People who have said words in a prayer without truly believing it and meaning it in their hearts and not being repentant of their sins, thereby not exhibiting a change in their lives, are not truly saved, but by their own choice. They choose Hell by their own choice. Just as the very popular, well-known verse of the Bible says, *For God so loved the world that He gave His one and only Son, that whoever believes in Him shall not perish but have eternal life.*[180] God desires that ALL would live in eternity with Him. So much so that He provided a way for that to happen. But He will not force any one of us to receive that free gift. He encourages, gives many opportunities, sends people to share the Gospel, and sometimes makes supernatural things happen for the good of people, to prove His

---

[179] Revelation 3:15&16

[180] John 3:16

love for them. But ultimately, we each have to make our own choice to receive His salvation."

She continued. "*Receive* is the key word. We must receive His free gift of salvation. We can't earn it, buy it, nor do we deserve it. God offers it freely and we must receive it by repenting of our sins and committing ourselves to Him and His way of living. Whether we do inwardly for His glory, and our good, and the increasing of the Kingdom, or we do it just to pretend we are, and to shut people up, and to look good speaking *Christian-ese* while sitting in a church, ultimately, God knows our hearts."

Stephanie added, "It's extremely important that we, as Christians, pray for those lukewarm people to get on fire for Christ and for revival to happen so that more would come to walk out what they only talk about. Too many continue living in sin and haven't expressed the fruit of being a follower of Christ. But how much more so should we pray for those who only assume they are saved because they acknowledge there is a God, and love Jesus and live out their lives in a 'good' way."

Raelene, sitting beside Stephanie, placed her hand over her cousins. Silence set in as everyone was deep in thought and retrospect.

"Is it possible to lose our salvation?" asked Reuben.

"Many theological arguments are had over this question. Who is right and who is wrong? Only God, who gave His Word knows. But as with everything, Papa and I go to the Bible and ask God to reveal His truths to us. I honestly believe that if someone who assumed they were saved and confessed they were Christian ends up in Hell, it's because they never really did fully commit from the beginning with their hearts. God speaks of it in the book of John when Jesus was walking into the Temple one day and the Jews surrounded Him asking, '*How long will you keep us in suspense? If you are the Christ, tell us plainly.*' Jesus answered them, '*I told you, and you do not believe; the works that I do in My Father's name, these testify of Me. But you do not believe because you are not of My sheep. My sheep hear My voice, and I know them, and they follow Me; and I give eternal life to them, and they will never perish; and no one will snatch them out of My hand. My Father, who has given them to Me, is Greater than all; and no one is able to snatch them out of the Father's hand.*' You see, we cannot be snatched out of God's hand, but we can choose to walk out of His hand."[181]

However, I do know that when we whole-heartedly and meaningfully go to Him and ask for forgiveness, we are instantly cleansed of our sin when we ask Jesus to forgive us and to become our Lord.[182] He does His part of welcoming us into His family as adopted children of the King—the Jews being His natural children; we as Gentiles, being His adopted children. He forgives us and we become washed clean of ALL of our wrongdoing and He chooses not to remember our sin any longer—Bonus![183] We are then free from sin and have a clean slate from which to start new life as a new creature in Christ, where old things have passed away and all things become new."[184]

"Then, we need to make a choice to learn of His Word and His ways and we have the free will to choose to live that out. Whether we do, or not, is our choice. If we choose to, there

---

[181] John 10:24-28

[182] 1 John 1:9

[183] Hebrews 8:12

[184] 2 Corinthians 5:17

will be proof of it in our 'fruit'. We will live out the Great Commission and go out and make disciples, not just get people to convert.[185] You cannot make disciples who live out the Word of God if you, yourself, don't know the Word of God and live it out in your daily life. God calls us to holiness. While no one is perfect and chooses the right way at all times and every single time, a follower of Christ will immediately feel remorse and will repent to Jesus, be forgiven, and move on making every effort not to sin in the same way again." explained Memaw.

"But God says He will not be mocked. We are saved by grace, but the Bible says we can fall from grace. *For in the case of those who have once been enlightened and have tasted of the heavenly gift and have been made partakers of the Holy Spirit, and have tasted the Good Word of God and the powers of the age to come, and then have fallen away, it is impossible to renew them again to repentance, since they again crucify to themselves the Son of God and put Him to open shame.*"[186]

"I believe this applies to those cases of turning from serving God to then serving Satan. When one that has loved Jesus, walked according to His Word, done deeds in His name as the Bible says we should, and then decides to renounce their faith in Jesus Christ and blatantly follow Satan instead, to the point of worshiping the devil—they lose their salvation, by their choosing."

"I can see that and how they lose their salvation in that situation," said Rueben.

"Losing your salvation doesn't happen without you knowing it. It's not going in and out of salvation in your walk. If you were

---

[185] Matthew 28:19&20

[186] Hebrews 6:4-6

never transformed at all to begin with, you probably never were born again from the start. And if you fell from grace, you were transformed and served Him, but knowingly and intentionally renounced Christ to then serve Satan," explained Memaw.

"Let's pray now, like Stephanie said, for the new Christians to grow strong; for the lukewarm Christians to get on fire for Christ; and for the unsaved to come to the knowledge of His saving grace and choose to receive His free gift of salvation," suggested Raelene.

"That no more Christians would renounce their faith in Jesus Christ and turn to worshiping the devil," said Stephanie.

"And for the seasoned Christians to make disciples, not just converts," added Matthew.

"And that Matthew not get cocky and have to be asked of God to quit building his muscles," laughed Reuben. The room erupted in laughter. Teasing Reuben for desiring to be as big as Matthew was given right back to him.

9.

ARMED AND PROTECTED

*"Put on the whole armor of God, that you may be able
to stand against the wiles of the devil."*
Ephesians 6:11

emaw and Olivia were caring for Annette, Addy and Luke while their four parents were at a meeting for their family business. The older siblings from both families were occupied other ways.

They were playing when Annette got rough with her words and Addy spouted out, "Stop being so mean, Jen-ni-ferrr."

Memaw walked in with a basket of clothes under arm, "Hey now, what's this all about, and who is Jennifer?"

"She's the bully in 4-H that is mean to the girls, especially me. Annette is acting just like her. She's not sharing. I want to play the game, too, but Luke and Annette hurried and got started to leave me out," whined Addy.

As the youngest child in her family of five, Addy was struggling to keep up with the 'big kids'. There are five years between Addy and Annette, the next child up from her, due to a miscarriage Andrea had. Five years apart makes a difference when you're six and eleven.

Memaw came around the center table where Annette and Luke played their game of Rummikub® "Have you got a hole in your armor, Addy?" She lifted Addy into her arms to comb her fingers through her hair and redo her ponytail and unruly braid. Addy was in need of some affection and loving on. Memaw was always ready to love on her grandkids.

"A hole in my armor? I'm not wearing any armor," said Addy.

"You're behaving as though you have a hole and allowed bitterness to take root and it's coming out toward others— whether they deserve it, or not."

"I don't understand. I'm not wearing any armor," said Addy, no longer patient.

"The armor I'm referring to is the armor of God from the Bible."[187]

"Ooh! *That* armor! Yeah, I know about that armor. Yeah, well, she started it," was all Addy said and was plenty content to defend her behavior with that.

"I know that you know what the armor of God does. Can you remind me?" asked Memaw. She tied the end of the braid with a thin, pink hair band.

"I know!" interjected Luke.

"I know, too." added Annette raising her hand.

"I know you two know. Actually, Addy knows as well. But it is Addy who's gonna tell us what all the elements of the armor do, right Addy?"

Having completely disregarded their game, Luke and Annette now turned their attention to Memaw and Addy's conversation.

---

[187] Ephesians 6:11

Olivia, having no clue what all this talk about armor was, also put down the book she was reading and listened for Addy's explanation.

"When we fight in prayer, we put on the armor of God so the devil can't attack us,"[188] answered Addy with a la-ti-da sing song voice to match the attitude.

"Good! You have the gist of the idea what the armor is for and aren't wrong, but we should wear the armor of God always, not just to do spiritual battle. Let's do this...Imagine in your mind's eye that we're putting on the full armor of God. Everyone, close your eyes and let's start at the bottom and put on your shoes of the gospel of peace first.[189] Come on, all of us," she included Olivia, Annette and Luke.

The children, together with Memaw, closed their eyes and began putting on imaginary shoes.

"Then the belt of truth.[190] This belt is more than a single strand that goes around the waistline. Belts during Bible times covered our entire middle section front and back, even hanging down to protect our thighs and a large portion of our legs," she explained.

All the children mimicked Memaw as they stepped into an imaginary belt and buckled it onto their waist.

"Next, let's put on our breastplate of righteousness,"[191] ordered Memaw as she pulled over her head a breastplate and put her arms through invisible arm holes.

"Then the helmet of salvation.[191] Are you imagining this?"

---

[188] Ephesians 6:10-13

[189] Ephesians 6:15

[190] Ephesians 6:14

[191] Ephesians 6:17

"Now let's pick up the shield of faith,[192] and we'll hold in our dominant hand the sword of the Spirit, which is, the Word of God."[193] She held up her right arm extending an imaginary sword.

"Does everyone have your armor on?"

Several responded, "Yeah."

"Yup, it's on," said Luke.

"Great. Okay, now that we're dressed let's stand in a position ready for battle. We must stand with our feet apart. Knees slightly bent, and have one foot slightly in front of the other so that we have a stance that is difficult to topple because we're centered and balanced."

"Feel it?" she asked. "Can you see it? You're strong and powerful, aren't you? You even look tough. You look scary to approach. You look like you could destroy!" grunted Memaw.

The children played into the description Memaw gave of what they looked like.

"Now keep your armor on, but don't stand as ready for battle as you had been. Stand straight and casual."

"No, no, keep your sword in your hand, don't ever put the Word of God down. Just stand relaxed but with your sword in hand," corrected Memaw as she saw hands come down to their sides.

"I feel like a guard outside a palace gate because while I am not in a battle stance, with all this heavy armor on, I can't hunch or feel relaxed and comfortable," said Annette playing into the imaginary game they were playing.

---

[192] Ephesians 6:16

[193] Ephesians 6:17

"Good! That is exactly the point I am trying to make. You just helped make my point, Annette. What I am saying in this illustration is, when you do spiritual battle in prayer, you arm yourself and stand in a defensive position that is ready to attack the Enemy and his demons with the word of God—just like Jesus did by saying, 'It is written!'[194] But even when you are not in a spiritual battle you should constantly have your armor on and stand tall holding the sword of the Spirit, or the word of God, ready for anything. You're ready to answer any question, any thought, any unexpected, stray, fiery arrow that comes out of nowhere because you are always armed with the Word and protected top to bottom."

The children listened with intent looks. They were taking it all in as they experienced the illustration.

"But when you take off the armor, you are neither protected, nor armed. You slump over or fall into a slouch that leaves you defenseless. This is how daily life is. Always be ready with your armor on, even when you are not doing battle spiritually. Always be ready to answer, with the Word of God,[195] any stray dart that is shot at you from someone's tongue. The only thing that should leave you, in action or in word, should be from the word of God," explained Memaw. "Let's try it!"

"Say you are sitting at the library and quietly reading a book on your own when some kid comes by and tells you, 'Move over, you're in my seat.' What should you do or say?" described Memaw.

---

[194] Matthew 4

[195] Psalm 119:41-46

Tell them, "I'm sorry, I was here first," said Luke with a smile, very pleased with himself that he'd been polite in his answer.

"While that is nicely spoken, thank you for being polite, Luke, that is not what the Bible says to do. The Bible says to give them the seat, and even offer your book."

Luke looked disappointed. Surely being nice and polite would have had to be the answer. No longer smiling, he felt embarrassed for having been wrong.

Memaw asked, "What would you do if, while playing at the park someone told you, 'You're so dumb, you don't even know how to play basketball.'?"

Reluctant to answer as not to be wrong, no one answered.

"The Bible teaches us that we are to smile at them and offer them a water bottle," she stated.

"Does it really say that?" asked Olivia, finding it hard to believe.

"It does say we are to give food and drink to our enemies and pour hot coals over their head," interjected Papa James. He walked in from the side door and went to the refrigerator for a cold drink.

Memaw smiled at Papa and nodded her agreement.

Papa thought he was throwing a wrench in her discussion but had actually helped her. It confused Luke and probably the others as in the same sentence it says to give your enemies life-sustaining food and drink and yet, pour hot coals over their head. Wouldn't that be hurting them, not blessing them?

"What!?" asked Addy. The children reacted with giggles, squirms, questions and silly comments about blessing people by being mean to them; Memaw was quickly losing their attention. She left the room for the kitchen and came back with a metal pan. Interested in what she was going to do with the pan, they quieted down to watch her.

Memaw went on to explain, "Proverbs 25, verses 21 & 22 says, *'If your enemy is hungry, give him bread to eat; And if he is thirsty, give him water to drink; For by doing so you will heap coals of fire on his head, and the Lord will reward you.'* "

Memaw poured imaginary coals from the metal pan she held over each their heads and it caused even more of a raucous. "Okay, back to our explanation so you understand the true meaning," she re-centered.

"In ancient Israel people used fire to warm up water, cook, and heat the house during the night. They needed coals to live and survive. Those coals were held in a brazier, or what is most commonly called a *fire pan*," she explained. "Now this isn't a real brazier or fire pan, but to give you an idea of what one would look like, it would be very similar to this," she showed them the metal pan.

"If a neighbor, or your family member, or friend came knocking at your door one night because they were out of coals would you share your life-sustaining coals with them so they could keep warm?" asked Memaw.

"Sure." piped up Addy.

"Yeah." exclaimed Luke.

"Yeah, I'd share," said Annette. "I could always just make more."

No answer came from Olivia, but she sat smiling.

Memaw smiled and continued, "I'm glad to hear you would graciously share with your friends, family or neighbors. But, would you share with your enemies?"

The responses weren't as quick to come. The children came around after thinking about it knowing it would be the right way to answer, but they did hesitate to be as willing to share as quickly with enemies.

"I would," stated Olivia resolutely, but only after a thoughtful pause.

"Yeah, I'd share," chimed in the others.

"It's only the right thing to do," said another, adding to the right spirit of the conversation.

"I'm glad to hear you would, because God's Word says, the Lord will reward you if you do take care of your enemies.[196] Giving your enemies food and drink and a brazier with hot coals is providing for their essential needs. That is love in action. God calls us to love all people, especially our enemies."[197] Memaw paused to allow those words to sink in.

She continued, "Even Peter encouraged us to repay evil with kindness to our enemies, *'Do not repay evil with evil or insult with insult, but with blessing, because to this you were called so that you may inherit a blessing.'*"[198]

"I want to share another story with you that isn't in the Bible. It's a little bit of a history lesson. When the United States was in the Civil War over abolishing slavery, President Abraham Lincoln told a group of guests at the White House that he planned to treat the South leniently after the war. 'Leniently' means to go easy on them. A visitor objected and said, 'But Mr. President, I would think you would want to destroy your enemies.' President Abraham Lincoln replied, 'Do I not destroy my enemies when I make them my friends?'"

---

[196] Luke 6:35

[197] Luke 6:27-29

[198] 1 Peter 3:8&9

With thoughtful looks on their faces, the children took in what Memaw shared about Abraham Lincoln as if to inventory their behavior toward the enemies they had been complaining about.

Memaw continued explaining that forgiving our enemies is so important to God that He includes it in His example of the way we should pray. "The disciples asked Jesus to teach them how to pray. Among many other great things, Jesus told them that they are to ask God to *forgive us as we have forgiven others*.[199] In another place in the Bible God says that *if we don't forgive others, he won't forgive us*.[200] He won't even listen to our prayers if we have unforgiveness toward anyone.[201] That is serious stuff. To forgive our enemies and love them are serious commands from God."

"That's hard to do when they're so mean," said Addy. She didn't appreciate the fact that she is to love when they hate and treat her so unkindly.

"They don't love on us." added Luke.

"God's ways are not our ways,"[202] added Memaw. "When others hurt us with their words, or actions we have a choice to make: bless their lives through acts of kindness and love, as God calls us to do; or, to be mean right back and take revenge. But God tells us very clearly that it is not for us to take revenge. *'Vengeance is mine, saith the Lord!'* "[203]

---

[199] Matthew 6:12

[200] Mark 11:25

[201] Proverbs 28:9

[202] Isaiah 55:8

[203] Romans 12:19

Jesus teaches with the following words written in red in the Bible, what does that mean? she asked.

Luke answered, "That Jesus spoke them."

"Yes. Jesus, Himself, said, 'people of the world say, *you shall love your neighbor and hate your enemy.* But I say to you, *love your enemies and pray for those who persecute you, so that you may be sons of your Father who is in Heaven.*'[204] He goes on to say a lot more about that but what I want to concentrate on is the fact that loving those who hurt us is not just a suggestion; it is a divine commandment from God. It is the second greatest commandment he gives. Does anyone know the first greatest commandment?"

"To love God with all your heart, soul and mind?"[205] answered Luke questioningly, not wanting to be wrong.

"Yes, Luke, excellent." acknowledged Memaw. "And the second greatest commandment is to love your neighbor as yourself—that includes neighbors that are enemies. That means that the same way you would take care of yourself, you should take care of your neighbor, yes, even your enemies are your neighbors. You need food, water, shelter, clothes and love and forgiveness and all good things—so does your enemy. You be the one to offer it to them."

She explained, "The Bible specifically says, *'Do not seek revenge or bear a grudge against anyone among your people, but love your neighbor as yourself. I am the Lord.'*[206] He says this in both the New Testament and in the Old Testament. He ends this commandment in the Old Testament by saying, *'I*

---

[204] Matthew 5:43-45

[205] Matthew 22:37-39

[206] Leviticus 19:18

116

am the Lord', to say that He has final say about it. He means it seriously. As THE Lord, He says this is how it will be. Follow it. Period."

"It's not easy to love my enemies when they don't like me so they don't want anything from me," said Addy, "I've tried to be nice."

"I understand, Addy. The truth is, Jennifer may not want to cave to your niceties in front of others. There's a saying, '*Hurt people, hurt people.*' We don't always know why someone is mean to others and why they want to hurt others, but usually, the most common reason is because they, themselves, are hurting and don't like something about themselves or their own lives. Bullies hurt others with their words or actions because they think it will make them feel better about themselves. If they are honest with themselves, it doesn't actually make them feel better to hurt others; but the devil wants to make them think it'll make them feel better to put someone else down to make themselves feel higher, stronger, better, overpowering. It's a false, self-lifting method."

"What if you try being nice to Jennifer when no one else is around?" suggested Memaw.

"I'm afraid to be around her when no one else is around. I try hard not to be alone with her," admitted Addy.

"That's a good thing if she gets physical with you, but if it's only verbal abuse Jennifer gives you, God is your strength."[207]

"You know you're not stupid. You know you're smart. You know you can take whatever she has to say to you because you are assured of who you are in Christ. She obviously doesn't

---

[207] Nehemiah 8:10

117

have that assurance or Jennifer wouldn't be treating others this way."

"You pray for strength to not believe anything mean she says to you or about you. And know that you know you are not what she is telling you. You have Jesus protecting you and you're wearing the armor of God. God's Word says in Psalm 18:48 *'He delivers me from my enemies; Surely You lift me above those who rise up against me; You rescue me from the violent man.'* " quoted Memaw.

"Pray beforehand that God would give you the opportunity and the words to tell her, even if not alone, but where no else can hear the love you show this child of God."

"God loves her too, just as much as He loves you. Jennifer doesn't know that. It might be that she does not feel love freely, or often," said Memaw very sympathetically.

"I know! I could give her the pack of gum Papa bought me at the store when I went with him." Addy said.

"That's a very nice and generous thing you want to do, but I would suggest you not give her anything material, or she may just come to you and force you to give her more material things. At least not yet, while she is still bullying you. Maybe later."

"What she really needs are words of affirmation. Those are words that mean something nice about her. Can you think of anything that is nice about Jennifer?"

Addy thought about it.

She thought some more.

It was actually a tough question.

After a long silence, "She has a nice smile even when she's teasing and being mean," answered Addy. She really had to dig deep.

"Good, tell her that. The moment after she says something mean to you, you say to her, 'You know, Jennifer, you actually have a really pretty smile.' Smile at her as you say it and keep on walking away. You'll throw her off her intended track of hurting you and you'll make her feel special instead."

Thinking about more, she added, "You might even just smile at her the next time you see her from far away. Intentionally try to make eye contact and smile. Making eye contact will let her know that you intend for the smile to be just for her and it is genuine."

With a deep sigh, Addy said, "Well, alright. I guess I can try it. I don't know that it'll work for someone who doesn't smile to be nice or happy. She only smiles when getting joy from being mean to someone or laughing at someone."

"I'm proud of you for wanting to try. I'll be praying for you, Addy. We all will, right kids?"

With a serious expression Luke asked, "Memaw, how can soldiers show love to people when they are at war with their enemies? They are your nation's enemies. You have to kill them before they kill you, but the Bible says not to kill."

"Very good questions, Luke, the Bible addresses that, too! The Bible has an answer to everything. As you well know, there are plenty of wars spoken of in the Bible. And there are wars being fought today. During times of war there is still opportunity to heap coals on and give life-sustaining needs to the enemy and their families."

"As for killing—you are referring to the Sixth Commandment that says, 'Thou shalt not murder'.[208] When you look up the verse in the original Hebrew language, the last word is translated

---

[208] Exodus 20:13

119

'murder', not 'kill'. Murder is done with premeditated fore-thought; with intent to deliberately take another person's life; to do evil harm. Murder is what you shall not do. Sometimes people have to kill in self-defense, or to save another person's life, or to stop an enemy before they destroy you or others."

"Even during times of war there are rules of engagement. You only attack if you are being attacked or your life is threat-ened. You only shoot someone that has a weapon in their hand aimed at you with the intention of killing you. It is wrong to shoot someone in the back. You don't hurt the women and chil-dren unless lives are in imminent danger because the intention of those women and children is to kill others—of which does happen, unfortunately. Those are all examples of ways that you heap coals on your enemies' heads," explained Memaw.

"But think about it from God's perspective," she continued. "While God promises rewards for giving love and forgive-ness and life-sustaining needs to our enemies,[209] He's always concerned about the souls of His children—all His children; your life and that of your enemies. It is His desire that we lead our enemies to Kingdom living, which brings with it eternal rewards for both you and that person."

"Along with receiving a reward for forgiving our enemies, we should be zealous for the salvation of our enemies. That we feed them the Bread of Life—Jesus—that they, too, may live a Godly life here and now, reaching others for the Kingdom too. I'm not saying that while they are spewing bad words at you that you tell them about Jesus' love for them right at that moment. But if you can soften their hearts slowly and eventu-ally with small acts of kindness, and nice words, showing them

---

[209] Proverbs 25:21&22

love over time, breaking them, the Lord will open up opportunity for you to share that Someone very Special loves them
with an unconditional love that is unlike any other love they
have ever received. As well as an opportunity at living a life
here on earth blessing others just as Jesus did. And, of course,
an eternal life in Heaven if they receive the free gift."

Memaw quickly added, "Now, I'm not saying it'll be easy.
I'm not saying that everyone will be open to receiving what you
share with them. And, I'm not saying that it'll happen right at
the moment you do share with them. The Bible talks about the
Word of God being a seed.[210] You may only be planting the Word
of God as a seed in their hearts today. God will send someone
else to water that seed, that means sharing more about Jesus."

"Maybe a nice neighbor lady of theirs will tell them of Jesus'
love for them?"

"Maybe one day in the future they accept an invitation to
attend a church service?"

"Maybe they have a Christian relative who speaks into their
lives of the love of Jesus?"

"Each time God sends someone to water the seed that you
sowed into their lives, they'll think back and remember that
you said something about Jesus and His love for them back
when they were in 4-H."

"We must pray for that to happen. God uses many people
at different times. But you play a part in that when you obey."

"Regardless of whether you plant the seed of the Word of
God, or God sends you to water the seed. You were used of

---

[210] Luke 8:11

121

God and each time you are, you're being rewarded by Your Heavenly Father in Heaven."[211] said Memaw.

"That was heavy. Let's lighten the mood and get a snack and you continue playing. I've gotta get cooking or we'll eat cheese and crackers for supper. Papa won't be too happy with cheese and crackers for supper," laughed Memaw.

Everyone ran to the kitchen to raid the pantry for a snack and the refrigerator for juice. Luke preferred milk.

Memaw called Luke over to privately encourage him.

"Mijo, I want you to know that it's okay to not know everything at all times. Learning and growing in the Word of God is a process. Even Papa and I, at this age, are still learning and growing. Things I had believed early on in my Christian walk to be understood one way, I am learning in my studies now, I had it wrong all along and I have to correct my way of thinking. It's an ongoing process to grow in His Word. The only time you should worry about it is when you are *not* growing. Then you need to be studying it out deeper or from right teaching, or ask Holy Spirit to reveal His Truths to you."

"I apologize if I hurt you when I corrected you. You had a very good answer, yes, but it wasn't the Biblical answer Jesus teaches to have made my point. But now you know the Biblical answer Jesus teaches and move on from here. There will be many more things to learn; you are only ten. But you're smart and willing to learn so it will come quickly. You won't ever know everything. Not any one person does," explained Memaw.

"Please don't get offended or discouraged when you learn that you understood something wrong. David said in Psalm 119:165, "*Great peace have they which love Thy law: and*

---

[211] 1 Corinthians 3:8

nothing shall offend them." He didn't say great peace have they that *know* Thy law, only that we have to **love** Thy law, and nothing shall offend us. But think about it...you have to know God's Word to be able to love it."

"Bottom line is, we shouldn't get easily offended when we love the law of God." With a great big hug and another apology Memaw squeezed Luke and kissed his head. He returned the gesture with warmth and asked for a lollipop from the jar.

"Not before supper, but good try," she winked.

Later that night, Memaw tucked Olivia into bed and pulling up the comforter over her, she bent low to kiss her cheek good-night. "Don't forget to say your prayers, Mija, I love you."

"Yes, Ma'am."

"Good night, Sweetheart," she switched off the light.

"Memaw?"

"Yes."

Olivia took a moment before answering, "Never mind."

"Mija, if you have something to say, please do."

"I don't."

"Okay. Good night then."

"Good night. I love you, too, Memaw."

Memaw smiled and prayed, "Soften her heart towards You, Lord. She needs Your forgiveness...and to forgive."

10.

WISDOM LEADS TO UNDERSTANDING

"Therefore the Lord said: Inasmuch as these people draw near with their mouths and honor me with their lips, but have removed their hearts far from Me, and their fear toward Me is taught by the commandment of men..."
Isaiah 29:13

Olivia walked into the kitchen with a mind running full of thoughts. She thought she wanted to ask a question, but wasn't really sure she wanted to know the answer. It might hold her accountable to her own actions.

She sat on a stool in front of the island where Memaw was chopping vegetables for supper.

Memaw smiled at her in greeting. She noticed Olivia fidgety.

Olivia stood and walked to the refrigerator and opened it. Closed it and walked to the pantry instead.

"Are you hungry? Supper should be done in about an hour," said Memaw.

"Memaw, I don't understand something, but I'm not really sure what it is that I don't understand. So, I don't know how to ask because I don't know what it is that I don't understand," said Olivia.

Memaw laughed.

Realizing how that sounded, Olivia laughed too.

"Okay. Let's start with what began the confusion."

"The other day, after Tyler's funeral, when we were talking about being saved and whether one could lose their salvation or not. I thought I understood what being 'saved' means, I guess I still don't. I know that you've said it is God's Kingdom living inside of us. I know you said we must make choices like Jesus would to show good fruit. I know you said we have to show His love to others. I get all that when you explain it, but it almost feels like I keep forgetting, or like I keep failing at it. Then I question whether I am truly saved at all," she admitted.

"I see," said Memaw, putting down the knife she was cutting with. She dried her hands on the dish towel. "Let's sit at the table."

Olivia added, "I don't know that I have said what I mean the right way. Why is this so confusing?"

"It's not confusing. It's actually simple. But I think what might be happening is you are battling how simple it is with what you thought, or assumed salvation to be. Let me ask you this, did you think we were supposed to be Christians so that life would be easier and God would bless us with what we ask for when we pray? That we wouldn't have any problems to struggle with and that we would never suffer any kind of hurt, or have need for anything?"

"Of course. Isn't it?"

"I thought so. Many Christians do think that. It's not that He doesn't want to bless us, or protect us and provide for us. It's more so that God is not a genie and Christians sometimes treat Him like one. We feel that because we are told in His Word we can go to Him for everything we need that He'll always answer as we ask Him to." Putting two glasses of tea before them, Memaw sat down and held Olivia's hands.

"When we're going through a hard time, we ask God to take away the difficulty of the situation for us so we don't have to suffer. We ask Him to heal us because we know He can. We ask Him to give us money because He is our Jehovah Jireh, our Provider. We ask Him to send us to a different school because the kids are so mean at our present school. We ask him to change other people because they make us miserable."

"Yeah, the Bible says we can pray for those things, but God doesn't always do them for us," answered Olivia, "Why not?"

"I can't pretend to know why, Honey, but I do know that our Heavenly Father is a good, good Father and He wants us to get more than just what we think is right for us to have."

"I'm not understanding," admitted Olivia.

"The Gospel is not a self-serving Gospel. It is a transforming Gospel that serves to make us like Jesus. He did not die a horrific death on the cross for us to have all our needs met, not even so that we avoid Hell. He died by being beaten to unrecognizable so that we would have the opportunity to be redeemed back to Him, just like He intended us to be from Creation, before Adam and Eve sinned. So that we could have fellowship with Him—to learn how to be like Him, to react like Him, and talk like Him, and treat others like He would. And, so that we would learn not to take offense when others hurt us with their words or actions. That is what a covenant relationship with God looks like."

She continued, "Instead, when God doesn't answer prayers like we think He should, we blame Him for not doing His part; we serve Him, after all. But honestly, it's that we're not doing our part."

"Okaaay," was all Olivia could say, still uncertain.

"Okay. There's a story in the Bible of a King who wanted everyone to bow down and worship an idol he'd made when they heard instruments playing music. Shadrach, Meschach and Abednego were three young guys that refused to bow down and worship any other god other than the One true God. So the king threw them into a big furnace blazing with fire to kill them for not worshiping his idol."[212]

Olivia looked up with big eyes, "Is this a true story?"

"It is. These three guys loved God, served God and trusted Him. Have you ever heard of this story?

"No."

"So, what do you think happened when God saw this?" asked Memaw.

"He put the fire out so they wouldn't get burned?"

"That's what most people want. For God to take away the problem we find ourselves in. But no, He didn't put the fire out."

"They burned to death?" asked Olivia, astonished.

"No."

"I don't get it, if God didn't put the fire out and they didn't burn to death, what happened?"

"That's the point I am trying to make, Sweetheart. Most people think that putting the fire out is the only right answer.

---

[212] Daniel 3:1-30

But God is much bigger than that and can do so much more than that. Let's not put Him in a box and restrict Him from working out bigger and better things through our circumstances than just immediately saving us from the pain that comes from our circumstances," said Memaw.

"True faith is trusting God in all circumstances. I'm talking about giving Him your problems entirely. Handing over every situation for Him to do what He feels is best for many involved, not only you—because Jesus teaches us to be selfless—so when we are selfless and willing to accept whatever His answer is, be it what it may, it works best for many people, not just one single person. Not just for you."

"That's hard to do," said Olivia.

"Not when you've learned to love and trust God and love others as you do yourself."

"Okay, that's where loving others comes in?" she asked with a smile creeping in with understanding.

"Right," whispered Memaw. "And when we believe the Gospel to be something other than what it really is—love like His—we reveal that we truly don't know God. Anyone who does not love, does not know God, because God is love."[213]

"That's another thing I'm confused over. Does that mean we can never get mad, or say something wrong, or do wrong things? Are we not saved if we do?" asked Olivia.

"Definitely not. When you do know God, you are more careful not to. Sometimes sin may happen, but when it does, you feel awful for having said that mean thing and immediately repent to God and ask for forgiveness from the person you said it to. When you do something wrong, Holy Spirit inside of you

---

[213] 1 John 4:8

is letting you know, 'that did not glorify God' and you desire to glorify Him in all things, so you repent of it and make it right immediately."

"Ooh, yeah, I see that," said Olivia, understanding better.

"You see, when you do love God and know what He says in the Bible, it's not easy to be mean or do wrong things. When you do, you immediately know it and make it right, and confess it to ask for forgiveness. It felt so wrong inside of you that you never want to do it again. And that's what living with the Kingdom of God inside of you looks like. You are different from who you once were, when doing and saying bad things never bothered you before. Make sense?"

"Yes, it does now," answered Olivia.

"When you live like that, you are obviously producing good fruit. And if you're producing good fruit, you must be a good tree, because bad fruit cannot come from a good tree.[214]

Olivia's countenance changed. She said in a low voice, "There are some Christians who produce bad fruit."

"They might not really have the Kingdom of God living in them. I can't say for sure, but look at all the Scripture that covers that. We, as His sheep hear His voice and follow Him.[215] When people are truly His disciples, they live in His Word and obey it.[216] If we have received Jesus as Lord, we are to walk in Him.[217] Those who keep His commandments know Him. If someone says they know Him but doesn't keep God's

---

[214] Matthew 7:18

[215] John 10:27

[216] John 8:31

[217] Colossians 2:6

commandments, the truth is not in them.[218] He is Truth and guides us into all truth,[219] remember?" explained Memaw.

"So then, they are not really saved, or they lost their salvation?"

"That's not for me to say, nor to pretend to know. Only Jesus has the right to judge that. I would venture to guess that they probably weren't saved at all or there would have been good fruit expressed. They would not be desiring to make bad decisions. And if they are saved, they don't really know the heart of God much and should learn His heart to express it, and to call themselves Christians," answered Memaw.

"Could they become a Christian, even after they thought they were, but aren't acting like one?"

"Definitely they can. And you should pray for them that they would make a sincere decision to be. That they'd surrender their lives to God so they could live transformed."

"Do you want to pray for them now?" asked Memaw.

"No."

"Okay," said Memaw, "but, Olivia."

Olivia looked up.

"I would be sure you stay right with God and forgive them, whoever this person is, so that your prayers are heard from God."[220]

Olivia looked down at her fingers as she rubbed her thumb.

"Here's another lesson about living as a Christian, Sweetheart. We have to believe what God says about who we are in Christ, and live that out. Don't believe what people say about us or our

---

[218] 1 John 3-4

[219] John 16:13

[220] Isaiah 59:2

situation. When people say or do things that make us feel badly, we have to remember who we are according to Christ. Otherwise, we believe people, instead of God. We must never allow people or life to dictate how we believe or act. We must only allow God and His Word to dictate what we believe and how we act. When we don't, we allow hurt, offense, hate and bitterness to enter us. When we do that, we cannot produce good fruit. If we truly believe who we are in Christ, we cannot be moved from that and we don't allow what people say to us or do to us ever move us away from who we are in Christ. We don't rely on people to say who we are. We only rely on who God says we are. His children.[221] Heirs with Christ.[222] Having authority over the evil one.[223] Holy because He is Holy.[224] Shining His Light.[225] Righteous, because righteousness is given us, through faith in Jesus Christ, to all who believe."[226]

With a croaky voice, Olivia said, "That's not possible."

"To believe that it's not possible, is believing a deceiving lie. That is what the devil wants. For Christians to hide behind the lie that 'everybody sins.' He whispers to us, 'You can expect to sin.' 'It's impossible not to.' 'We are not holy enough, only Jesus is Holy.' 'Nobody's perfect.' Those are all deceiving lies from Satan."

---

[221] 1 John 3:1

[222] Romans 8:17

[223] Luke 10:19

[224] 1 Peter 1:16

[225] Matthew 5:16

[226] Romans 3:22

"Either you believe God's Word, or you don't. This is all about dying to self. We must crucify our flesh,[227] Olivia. That means, put to death what feels 'right' to us. Put to death what we will for ourselves. Put to death what we struggle with in our flesh. We're to put on Christ and His robe of righteousness."[228] answered Memaw.

"I guess I believe it when you explain it. But then I go about my day and something happens, or somebody says something and I fall back into old thoughts."

"And Jesus knows that, which is why the Bible says we are to work out our own salvation with fear and trembling.[229] Work out that old creature we used to be. He gives many scriptures that help us cast down those thoughts that don't line up with what He says.[230] He gives us scriptures that say he helps us when we are tempted.[231] He gives us scriptures that say we are to set aside every weight and sin that easily drags us down and run the race that is set before us with endurance."[232]

"So it *is* possible to learn how to and that is called, *working out our salvation*?" wanting to be sure she understood.

"That's right, Honey. See, you do understand."

Olivia stopped tracing the outline of the napkin holder at the center of the table and looked up, "You never did say how God helped those three guys in the hot fire."

---

[227] Galatians 5:19-24

[228] Romans 13:14 & Isaiah 61:10

[229] Philippians 2:12

[230] 2 Corinthians 10:5

[231] 1 Corinthians 10:13

[232] Hebrews 12:1

"Oh, yes. The Bible says there appeared a fourth person in the fire. In Hebrew, the number four is Dalet. Dalet means 'a door'. 'The Door' is one of the many names of Jesus because He is the doorway to the Father.[233] So, Jesus was the fourth man that appeared in the fire with Shadrach, Meshach and Abednego."[234]

Olivia's eyes grew wide.

"Yeah, so you see. God doesn't always get us out of our bad situation; however, He walks through it with us."

"Wow," is all Olivia could say.

"That's not all. The three guys stepped out of that flaming furnace without so much as the smell of smoke on their clothes. Nothing burned. Not even their hair was singed!"[235]

Amazed, Olivia said, "Now that's what I call a miracle."

"Yeah, and that's still not all. The king then said, 'Blessed be the God of Shadrach, Meshach and Abednego.' And he made a decree throughout the land that if anyone spoke against their God, they would be torn limb from limb. 'No other god is able to deliver like their God,' said the king.[236]

"Nahhh," said Olivia, in disbelief.

"That's right, even the king came to acknowledge the one and only true God after that.[237] Do you think that would have happened if God would've put out the fire to rescue them?"

"Probably not."

---

[233] John 10:9

[234] Daniel 3:25

[235] Daniel 3:27

[236] Daniel 3:28-29

[237] Daniel 4:2-3

"Probably not. You see how God is interested in helping more than just His children in trouble? Greater work can be done, and for more people, when God does things His way instead of in our limited way."

"Yeah, I get that."

"So, what would you say is the moral of the story?"

"Trust that God loves me and will help me. Don't tell Him how to do His job, or my situation won't be helping as many other people as possible. It's not only about me," answered Olivia.

"That's pretty good, Sweet Girl. You do understand, after all."

They laughed together.

11.

FROM VICTIM TO VICTOR

"...I have written to you, young men, because you are strong,
and the word of God abides in you, and you have
overcome the wicked one."
1 John 2:14

Michael is Memaw and Papa James' grandson from Marissa. He's a hard-working young man that's been with the same construction company since he was sixteen years old. He has a heart for ministering God's love to people. Michael always has a smile on his face and rejoices over what the average person can oftentimes subconsciously and inadvertently take for granted. Michael loves life and sees the beauty of God's creation in the small things.

To someone who is unhappy and discontent with their life and has a negative outlook on most things, personalities like Michael's could get on their nerves. Michael works with such a person as this by the name of Roger. Roger had a difficult home life growing up. His mother abandoned his father with three small children. Having been the eldest of the three, Roger carried the weight and responsibility of caring for his younger sister and brother. After his father came to terms with the realization that his wife wasn't going back and having battled depression for many months, his father took his own life. He didn't want to live without his wife and was overwhelmed by the burden of having to raise three young children by himself.

For almost two months Roger managed to keep his siblings fed with what was in cupboards and then resorted to stealing food before Child Protective Services were notified. The school called CPS when he had not been in attendance and every phone call home was answered by a message that the number had been disconnected. A call to CPS was also made by the landlord who several times knocked on the door to collect rent. Roger lied about his parents' whereabouts many times before the landlord realized he lived there by himself with his sister and brother. To avoid the children getting placed in the foster care system their grandmother took them in but that only lasted two years before the grandmother passed away from a lost battle to cancer. Unfortunately, during the two years that he lived with his grandmother the older neighbor boy the children kept company with abused Roger in unthinkable ways.

After their grandmother's death, CPS took the children from her home and placed them with three different foster families. Roger never again saw his siblings. He never found out what kind of lives they lived, or if they lived. His life was a torrent of ugliness, trouble, and placement in home after home. He never was placed with a family that would show him love, acceptance and encouragement that every growing boy needs.

For Roger, to see Michael a happy, fortunate and blessed young man only brings out the anger of how unfair life is. He hates Michael for the happy person he is and he makes the

Monday through Friday work days a miserable time for all people he works with.

The family is gathering at Memaw and Papa James' farm to celebrate Addy's baptism, one of Michael's little cousins. He is helping set up tables and chairs out in the ramada beside the garden and Memaw is cleaning the outdoor sink and counter area.

"How are you, Mijo? How's the little gal you're praying about dating? How's work? Tell me about you. I miss you," asks Memaw, to catch up with her grandson.

"All is good. Samantha and I are still talking and getting to know one another. I haven't made any decisions, yet, if I officially ask her dad to court her or not. I really want to know from the Lord that it's His will," said Michael.

"I got a new bar light for my truck that'll look really cool. I want to ask Papa to help me install it," he shared with excitement.

"I know he'd love to help you install your new light," she answers with a smile. Michael needs no instruction at all to get the job done, he is quite capable with tools and installations of that kind. The fact that he wants Papa's help is solely for the time spent together.

"It warms my heart you're going to the Lord for guidance and not moving on your own, Mijo," smiles Memaw, touching his arm. "She's a sweet girl. Will she be..."

Before Memaw could finish asking if Samantha would be attending the baptism, they are interrupted by a crash. They stop setting up tables and run.

Michael arrived before Memaw. The loud crash was a ladder that had fallen. Papa James was up on a ladder, stringing lights from the house to the pump room that would eventually lead to the ramada so that there would be lighting once the sun goes down. He'd lost his footing and the ladder toppled. Papa was hanging from the overhang of the roof. John and Ethan arrive at the same time, as everyone who hears the commotion runs to the sound from where it came. Papa had many witnesses of his misstep on the ladder.

"Lose something?" asks Ethan, picking up the ladder.

"How strong are you, ol' man?" added John while helping Ethan center the ladder under Papa's feet. Both men teasing and laughing once they knew all was well.

Papa's a strong man that holds his own, but it sent Memaw's heart racing to see him dangling there, nonetheless. The point he is hanging from is near the peak of the roof, not the shorter end toward the porch.

"Not as strong as I used to be, that's for sure," answers Papa wiping his brow with the back of his trembling hand, laughing at himself with the others. In comes Memaw for a hug and to be sure he is alright. She whispers in his ear, "Did you hurt anything?"

"Nah, I'm fine. Still got it!" he answers with a smile, kissing her lightly on the cheek, then heads back up the ladder to finish the work.

Memaw rolls her eyes and shakes her head.

"I'll finish out here, Memaw," offers Michael, "You go inside and get out of the heat."

"Thank you, Mijo, I will." She needed to settle her racing heart and check on her beans.

Memaw puts water to boil. She pulls out veggies that needed chopping for the salad and serves herself a glass of water. In walks Tommy, Marissa and Michael with heads bowed and worried expressions on their faces.

"Momma, Tommy and Michael are headed into town to help a friend. They'll be gone for a while but Ethan's taking over the work Tommy was doing and I'll take over the decorating that Michael was doing," explained Marissa.

"Oh, okay, of course, yeah, do what you need to do," she answered, with a look of concern. It is evident from the looks on their faces that something is not right.

"Michael, may I tell Memaw? We really should pray for Roger," asked Marissa.

"Definitely, thank you, yes, he needs prayer."

"Roger. Isn't that the name of the young man that gives you a lot of trouble at work and doesn't like you much?" she recognized. "Papa and I have prayed for him before, right?"

"You two go on ahead and keep me posted. I'll fill Memaw and Papa in and we'll be praying. Stay safe. God bless you and help you," said Marissa.

After hugs Tommy and Michael walk out. Memaw calls out to them, "You bring that boy back here and we'll get him fed and loved on."

Her love for all makes Michael smile. "Yes ma'am."

"This poor kid just got arrested for rioting and looting," explained Marissa. "Apparently, it started out as what was supposed to be a peaceful protest, but it got out of hand, obviously."

"Oh no." expresses Memaw. "Why don't you call your dad in and we'll pray. We can't let this go without praying. Then we'll all get back to work for the baptism."

Marissa went outside to look for Papa. Memaw began to pray for Roger, and for Tommy and Michael who were walking into the situation. Marissa must have filled him in with the details because they walk into the kitchen and Papa says, "Let's go to the bedroom, we'll get this covered in prayer."

As Memaw, Marissa and Papa head to the bedroom on a mission, they pass Laura and Andrea. The two look at one another and join the train headed down the hall.

Marissa explains that they are gathering in the bedroom to pray for a kid Michael works with named, Roger. "He's been arrested for looting after what started as a protest broke out into a riot. He called Michael with his one phone call so Tommy and Michael are headed into town to see if they're allowed to pick him up from the Sheriff's Department."

"Oh no," said Laura, "That is terribly sad."

"We'll join you in praying," said Andrea.

Papa started, "Heavenly Father, with hearts that rejoice over all You've done for us, we thank You for all that You are, and all that we are in and through Your Son, Jesus. Because You are faithful and just, we lift up Roger to You and ask that his heart would be softened toward the Love You are and have to offer him. Please be a present help to him in his time of trouble. May He feel You near him and desire to know from where his help comes. May Tommy and Michael be allowed to talk with him and somehow get him out of that jail cell. We ask that You'd please prepare a way to minister to this young man that he would be open to hearing the Gospel shared with him. Open his ears and his heart to receive the Good News of Your Son, Jesus. It's in His name, the name above all names, we pray. Amen."

"Amen!" agreed the four ladies out loud in unison.

"Please stay in prayer for this kid, and for Michael and Tommy's safety, too," asked Marissa, choking up a bit.

Andrea and Laura on either side of Marissa agree to pray with a threesome hug. "Keep us informed as you hear news?" asks Laura.

"Definitely."

Everyone headed back to work for the celebration. Walking out arm-in-arm, Memaw squeezes Marissa's hand. "Everything will be alright," she reassures.

"Thanks Momma. I gotta get the centerpieces set up and then I'll be in to help you with the salad," she forced a smile.

Outside, everyone is scurrying around working, laughing, joking and playing as finishing touches are being wrapped up for the baptism and celebration. Ethan is filling the water trough that had been brought to the courtyard from the barn — in it is where Addy is to be baptized by her daddy and Papa James. Reuben, Benjamin and Matthew are setting up the sound system. The younger children are running around playing. The ladies are in the kitchen cooking.

Finally, it is time for the ceremony. "Please gather around," asks John. He starts by asking Addy if for sure and for certain she knows Jesus as her Lord and Savior and what that means to her.

Addy responded, "Yes, Daddy, I surrendered my life to Jesus last month at Bible Camp. I know I did because when I asked Him to forgive me of my sins, I felt His love and forgiveness right away; I cried because it made my heart feel clean and light. Now, I think of Him when I do things."

"Good, Addy, I'm proud of you," said John kissing her cheek with tears in his eyes. With that, John on one side of the trough with one hand on Addy's back and the other pinching her nose closed; and Papa on the other side holding her hands, John said, "Papa and I baptize you in the name of God the Father, Jesus Christ and Holy Spirit." Down into the water she went and back up again to the sound of cheers and applause and whistles. John lifts her up and out of the trough while Andrea, through tears, wraps her in a hug with a large white towel and picks her up to hold her tight and whisper praises to God.

Marissa is lost in the special moment, feeling gratitude over her niece's decision, when she feels her phone vibrate in her pocket. "Hello," she answers turning her back to the group to walk away from the noise of the celebrating crowd.

"Mom, do you think it'd be alright if we brought Roger to Memaw's and Papa's with us? Dad posted his bail. I really don't want him going home to an empty apartment and I don't want him to go back out to the streets. Do you think Tio John and Tia Andrea would mind him being at Addy's party?"

"Yes, Mijo, absolutely bring him. You heard Memaw, she wants to feed him and love on him," she smiled.

"Okay, thanks, we'll be there in an hour."

Marissa informed them all that Tommy and Michael were on their way back and they will be bringing Roger with them.

"Oh good!" said Memaw.

"Of course!" said Andrea.

Papa only nodded his head in agreement.

An hour and forty minutes later they finally arrive. Tommy whispers to Marissa with a kiss on the cheek, "We stopped by Michael's so Roger could change. He was uncomfortable coming knowing there was a party going on."

She smiled and hugged Tommy, "I'm just glad you're all here now."

To the guests, it appeared as Michael brought a friend to the party. It was only the immediate family that realized Tommy and Michael had disappeared for a while.

Roger quietly shook hands but didn't smile much as Michael went around introducing him as his friend and co-worker. Memaw was quick to bring them all a plate of warmed food and hugged the three upon the introduction to Roger.

"You can call me Memaw, everyone else does," she smiled.

"Thank you," said Roger.

Pushing his food around some and only taking a few bites, Roger didn't appear to be hungry, or didn't like the carne con chile with a kick. He was quick to finish the tortilla.

It was late and guests were saying their goodbyes, thanking John and Andrea for the invitation. What was left of the cake had already been taken inside. For the most part, the immediate family were the only ones left, but that made quite a crowd even still. The children were off playing. The teenagers were around a fire Reuben had built, and the adults were visiting with some beginning to clean up. It left Roger and Michael sitting at a table in the back corner of the ramada by themselves.

Roger, looking up at Michael sitting across the table from him asks, "Why are you doing all this?"

Olivia approached and sat beside Michael. She was usually welcomed by all the cousins because she was quiet and not annoying. Michael smiled at her. She'd heard Roger's question. Quietly, she traced the outline of the horseshoe that sat as part of the table's centerpiece allowing Michael to answer him.

"Doing what?"

"This," pointing to his food and gesturing around. "You've brought me to your grandparent's home. You're feeding me.

I'm wearing your shirt. You bailed me out of jail, for God's sake, why?" asked Roger.

"Like you said, 'for God's sake.' I'm supposed to do good to others,"[238] answered Michael.

Roger sat seething, unable to understand why he was being treated as an important guest, knowing full well how he treats Michael at work. He doesn't even like Michael. And all this makes him mad because he doesn't *want to* like him. He resents the fact that now he owes Michael and his dad for bailing him out of jail. All these thoughts and uglier ones were rolling through his head.

Olivia, very out of character, broke the silence and asked, "May I ask you a question?"

"I didn't steal anything," Roger spat out.

"That's not what my question is about," answered Olivia. "I'm just curious, why'd you call Michael when you could've called anyone else from jail?"

Roger dropped his head and sat silent, blinking fast.

"Maybe because you knew he'd help you?" asked Olivia.

"I had no one else to call, I have no family," he mumbled.

"I'm glad you called me, man," answered Michael, trying to deflect the embarrassment he knew Roger felt over his confession.

"But why would you help me, you know I don't even like you. I'm never nice to you and make work he--...heck for you," he corrected himself looking up at Olivia barely caring that he almost cussed in front of a child.

"Roger," said Olivia, "I think that deep down you do like Michael, but don't want to, nor like the fact that you do. You

---

[238] Matthew 7:12

definitely don't want to give him the satisfaction of knowing that you might like him. You might show him disrespect, but you have to be around him to be able to show him that you don't care for him."

Roger glared, "Who do you think you are, telling me how I feel?"

"Easy, man, she's just a kid," defended Michael.

Roger didn't like, nor appreciate, someone telling him how he felt—especially a kid. He wouldn't have put it in those words, exactly, but was struggling to deny those truths to himself. There was no way he was going to admit those feelings out loud, that was for sure. He stared down at his plate of food.

Michael wanted to silence Olivia, but knew she'd hit a chord, and for lack of a better explanation, he felt he needed to allow her to speak. She did, after all, have a lot in common with Roger and thought, *maybe she can penetrate his hardened heart?*

"I get it," said Olivia. "We baked cookies together with all the cousins and every time I rolled out my dough it would break on me. He calmly and patiently does what I get aggravated over and I get angry with myself over being aggravated. I don't like to be reminded of what I can't do well," admitted Olivia.

Matthew smiled without looking up, thinking back to the time she was referring to.

Roger looked up to meet Olivia's gaze and could only think, *are you actually agreeing with me?*

Wait. Roger re-centered. *No, she's actually pointing out **my** shortcomings. Wait a second. Who does this kid think she...*

Roger's thoughts were stopped short by Olivia's next words.

"I figured out it's not what Michael does wrong that I don't like. It's what Michael represents and reminds me of that I don't have, nor are, that I don't like," paused Olivia. "At least that's what it was for me," she said, shrugging her left shoulder, matter-of-factly.

Roger sat in silence to hear his own heart's feelings coming from another.

"You think you know me? Kid, you have no idea about my life."

"No, I don't, but I do recognize your attitude about life. Not everyone but you, has it easy. Others suffer too. I'm not saying you don't have reason to be angry with how your life is. But I've learned it's how you choose to handle the circumstances that make you who you want to be. Believe it or not, you can choose to use your circumstances to make you stronger and helpful to other people in a useful way," she encouraged. "Memaw taught me that."

"Ha-ha," chuckled Roger looking doubtful and tired of this cheerleading conversation from a kid, no less. "I don't have a single thing that could be useful or helpful to anyone. Kid, you don't even know. How could you? Look at all this," stretching out his hand toward the yard and family that surrounded them. "It's easy for you to sit there and pretend that I have things to be thankful for when you're surrounded by a big, fancy house and all this family that loves you. Look at all the things you have. You have no clue what hard life is."

"Roger, you assume I've had a good life because of what you see. You mistake what you see for what really is. The same way I don't know about your life, you don't know about mine. Because you see me sitting here with Michael and he welcomes me you assume I've always had him as family and that I've never had it bad. When, up until nine months ago I was an orphan in foster care. I came to live with Memaw and Papa after I was arrested for breaking and entering because I was starving and alone. I was being abused in the home I was in and had been for as long as I could remember."

"I'm not the only one who has suffered. Memaw's father left her without a daddy and committed suicide." Olivia continued, "You see that kid jumping off the tractor over there? This family prayed God would keep him alive and make the surgery work as he had open heart surgery. This house you see as fancy has all things used—either given to them, hand-made or bought second-hand. Memaw and Papa have had children disobey and choose to do things they didn't believe were right. They pray their grandchildren through tough struggles. No one here is perfect—especially, not me. But I've learned from Memaw, and this family, that the choices we make for our lives are what make us joyful—or not. But we each have to choose. I learned to be grateful my life isn't worse than it was because it could *always* be worse. I know."

Roger was quiet for what felt like half an hour—even though it probably wasn't even a full minute that went by. He was thinking through all that Olivia had just said. It wasn't only Roger doing some thinking. Michael, too, was deep in thought about Olivia's words. He didn't actually set out to have a good attitude all the time. He was just wired that way. That's why he didn't understand when people didn't like him for it. It wasn't anything he was doing for attention, to act righteous, or to be the favorite one. He just didn't think any other way other than to be grateful and content in all things, most times.

No one had realized when Papa and Memaw had arrived. They were standing behind Michael and Olivia when Roger looked up at Memaw and asked, "So your dad committed suicide too?"

"He did," she simply answered.

What began with a whisper escalated into a full out raging question in anger, "What do you even do with that? How am I supposed to forgive him for being so selfish and leaving me to take care of my siblings without his help? My mom had already abandoned us. He left me with no one! He doesn't have the excuse of an accidental death. He doesn't have the excuse of someone making that choice for him by taking his life. He wanted to leave us! He chose to leave us! Just like she did!"

"May I hug you, Roger?" asked Memaw.

No answer came.

Of course, she took that to mean *yes,* so she stood behind him and wrapped her arms around him and wept for him. Everyone around teared up. Everyone but Roger.

After a few minutes of tearing and holding him, Memaw wiped her eyes and blew her nose into the tissues that Michael handed her. She finally spoke.

"Roger, there's a verse in the Bible that says, God is the father to the fatherless and a husband to the widows.[239] I got great comfort in that but not just by hearing it. It took really getting to know how much God truly loves me and all He did for me, just like a good daddy, for me to receive that comfort. Can we share with you all that God has done because He wants to be your Daddy?" she asked.

"I know where you're going with that. My grandma would occasionally take my brother and sister and I to church but she was too sick to take us often. Then, she died. How can I accept a God that would allow so much bad to happen? That's not love. That's not protecting your own. Why didn't He stop the

---

[239] Psalm 68:5

abuse? Why didn't He provide for us? Why didn't He keep us together to begin with?"

Memaw looked him straight in the eyes to answer, "It isn't God who caused those bad things to happen. That was evil and wrong and only the devil is behind bad things that happen.[240] God's intention was for His children to live out joyful, pleasant, blessed lives. But sin entered the world through Adam and Eve and dominion over the earth was given over to the devil. Those bad things happen because we live in a fallen world. But we have hope. God made provision for us to take that authority and dominion back from the devil. You know the popular Bible verse that says, *'For God so loved the world that He gave His only begotten Son, that whosoever believes in Him should not perish, but have everlasting life.'*?"[241]

Roger nodded that he recognized it.

"Yes, well, because offering animal sacrifices for our sins would only cover them temporarily, God made a way that our sins could be forgiven for good and for always. He sent His Son, Jesus, to be the final sacrifice for our sins. When we receive The Gift He's given us, we are not only forgiven of our sins after we ask to be, but we are given the authority over the devil to stop him from working in our lives. Oh, he'll still attempt attacks, but if we stand strong and use God's Word against him, like Jesus did, and if we speak God's promises over our lives and we live out God's Word in our deeds and speech, we will prevail over the Enemy from working in our lives. But we have to *know* God's Word to do battle in the Spirit against the Enemy's attacks."

---

[240] John 10:10

[241] John 3:16

Roger didn't look up at Memaw while she spoke to him until she told of a way to have authority over the devil's attacks.

"What you see and perceive as Michael being a goody-two-shoes and our family as being 'good' or 'having it all' is nothing more than our living out the Word of God. We are happy, but only because we recognize who we are in Christ and all that we have been saved from. We are rich, but only because we value everything as being a gift from God, not by the price tag of the items."

Memaw further explained, "Roger, when you're confident of who you are in Christ nothing should bother you, offend you, or move you as to *who you truly are*. You learn to see how many of life's experiences—good and bad—truly can be used to glorify God and for the good of others. Nobody can take anything from you unless you give it. That includes your dignity, your honor, your integrity, your position as a child of the Most High God. You see, not your race, not the color of your skin, not the amount of money you make, not physical or mental impediments, nor the neighborhood you live in dictates who you are. When you are a child of the Most High God, it doesn't matter if you were raised on an island, are purple, eat peanut butter and grasshoppers every day for every meal, and fly everywhere you go. Nothing makes you different than every other person God has created, other than what *you allow* differences to be."

"You are, by no means, the only one who has had hard-knocks in life. And it is not race, color, physical handicap, whether affluential or impoverished, nor the area of town you live in that determines whether you get more, or less knocks. Each knock down, each experience, and each incident could be used for good. Everything that the devil intends for evil, God can use for good.[242] You cannot know how many times I've been able to comfort others when I share that my dad committed suicide. Instead of using that experience I had to go through as a crutch in my life, I've chosen to use that as a tool to minister love and help others get through their experiences with suicide. We've been able to help others get through tough situations because we've been in tough situations ourselves.[243] Instead of living sad that I had a child die, I look forward to meeting that Baby in Heaven and getting to know him. We named him, Angel Baby, by the way," she smiled.

Memaw went on, "God created you to be His child. He loves you and does protect you and provide for you. So much so, that He's made a way for you to live like Jesus lived on this earth. He has provided a way for you to have a family surrounding you when you attend a church consistently as he calls us to congregate with other believers.[244] He has provided a means to fight off the devil with His Word.[245] He has provided a way for us to be healed of infirmities and hurts.[246] He teaches us how to handle those who mistreat us and do us wrong.[247] And, He has provided a way for us to have eternal life."

"We cannot cry and feel sorry for ourselves to the point that we cripple ourselves from living. We cannot blame our life experiences for being angry, bitter and resentful toward others today. We have the choice to use those bad life experiences to

---

[242] Genesis 50:20

[243] 2 Corinthians 1:3-6

[244] Hebrews 10:25

[245] James 4:7

[246] Isaiah 53:4

[247] Matthew 5:43-45

bless and help others. To caution others. To make sure that we don't make the same mistakes twice. To see to it that our future children and their children aren't stuck in what our choices were. To use what we learn from our experiences for good, not for evil. To grow from them and use them to motivate us toward the betterment of our lives and of those around us."

Papa chimed in, "Roger, we are what the world calls 'minorities' too, but we don't live like we are minimized because of a label. If we lived according to what others thought of us, or what their expectations of us are based on their perceptions or opinions, we'd lose out on being who God sees us as. We cannot change others' opinions or perceptions or prejudices. We can learn who God calls us to be and live that out to the fullest. In so doing, it should never matter who thinks differently of us, or what is thought of us at all. It doesn't even matter how we're treated. We know that we know we are loved and that we are children of the Almighty who created us and loves us and defends us. That is enough. We are immovable because of that knowledge."

Michael added, "And when we're treated badly by others, we continue doing what the Bible says to do. We love unconditionally,[248] we give our enemies food and water, and we turn the other cheek.[249] That's why I went for you today and why my dad posted your bail."

Roger looked deep into Michael's eyes still not understanding how he could show such compassion when Roger treated him so badly. These people live what they believe. That is what makes them different. Without meaning to. Without

---

[248] 1 Corinthians 13:3-8

[249] Proverbs 25:21 & Matthew 5:39

wanting to. Without even trying, Roger's heart began to soften all on its own. It felt good to allow kindness and love in, and not have to keep walls up to protect himself. There wasn't anything he needed to protect against at this moment. And for now, it felt freeing.

The deep conversation was interrupted by little Addy as she came around with a basket full of candy and offered some to Roger first, then Olivia and the others.

"I will gladly take it if it's chocolate," answered Memaw.

"It is chocolate. Your favorite." Addy smiled and leaned in for a cuddle.

"Thank you," answered Roger with the first hint of a smile that evening.

"How about we break this up and get the help of strong, young men to put up all these tables and chairs while we have them available? Otherwise, we'll have to do this by ourselves tomorrow," suggested Papa.

"Yes, sir," stood Michael to his feet.

"Yes, sir," said Roger, as he stood and followed suit, almost like one of the family.

Memaw placed a hand on Roger's arm to get his attention, "One last thing, please know you have a family in us. And don't forget that LOVE changes things. God is Love.[250] I encourage you, take the time to learn of His words in the Bible and live them out. This is the only way to change the cycle of oppression and the victim mentality that Satan uses in the minds of so many who consider themselves less than. It isn't necessarily that others *always* make people feel less than, although yes, there are people who do make others feel this

---

[250] 1 John 4:16

way, both intentionally and some subconsciously. Nevertheless, more often than not, an attitude of 'I am owed for what I've had to endure for being...' whatever...you fill in the blank. Many would fill it in with 'being poor', some with 'handicapped', others with 'being Black' and yet others with 'having a mental disability', or 'being Mexican', and many other reasonings we can continue to list out, for there is no lack of hurting people for various reasons."

"But think on this," Papa added, "Jewish people went through horrible persecution and were dispersed out of Rome in 70 A.D. Six million Jews were murdered during the Holocaust. And later, two-thirds of the Jewish people will be killed in the coming Tribulation by the Anti-Christ. And Jewish people are God's chosen people. We are Gentiles. We are only adopted into God's family. Jews are His first and chosen children. Stop and think for a moment how that must make God feel? Do you know why all that happened to God's chosen people? The Bible says, 'The Gentiles shall know that the house of Israel went into captivity for their sin; because they were unfaithful to Me...' "[251]

Papa concluded with, "Have you sinned? You don't want to be separated from God. No one is exempt. And God will not force Himself on anyone. We all have the choice. What choice will you make?"

Memaw looked deep into Olivia's eyes with a smile that said, *'I'm proud of you.'* She squeezed her tight. Olivia knew what she meant without a word. It did feel pretty good to help someone else for a change.

---

[251] Ezekiel 39:23

12.

NEVER ALONE

"Whenever I am afraid, I will trust in You."
Psalm 56:3

"Yes, Linda, it'll be alright. Please know we'll continue in prayer. Let me know if there is anything I can do for you." Memaw hung up the phone after having prayed with the neighbor, Mrs. Madrid. Her son and their dog were lost. They had gone for a walk down their road but hadn't come back home. It had been over four hours since they left. Papa and Daniel went out to help Mr. Madrid look for 9-year-old Ben and his dog, Boots.

Because Daniel and Cynthia with their three children were over for supper that evening, the kids were happily playing outside until they heard the news of Micah's little buddy, Ben. Now they remained inside where it felt safe.

"Mom, can I please go help Dad and Papa look for Ben? I want to help. I promise to stay with them," asked Micah.

"They've already left, Micah, I can't have you out there alone not knowing which direction they headed in. You'll just have to sit tight and wait here until we hear from them. I may drive you to them once they report in. Until then, just pray for Ben, Honey," answered Cynthia as she continued washing supper dishes.

Memaw asked if the children wanted to make cookies.

"I don't feel much like eating cookies right now, but thank you," answered Ezra.

Stephanie said, "I can't seem to concentrate on much of anything else right now."

Micah only stood at the window.

Olivia smiled at Memaw.

Memaw felt some relief. While she didn't want to alarm the children with her own worry for Ben, she really didn't feel much like baking. *What could we do to distract the children from worrying about Ben and Boots?* she thought.

"I prayed with Ben's momma, but how about we continue in prayer for Ben and Boots? That's the best help we can give," she suggested.

The children followed her into her bedroom. She prayed throughout the house, but serious prayer was mostly done in her praying chair.

As the kids climbed onto Memaw and Papa's bed, Memaw settled into her chair, placing her cup of tea on the table where her Bible lay.

Ezra asked, "Do you think Ben will have to sleep outside?"

"Ahhh," smiled Memaw looking up. "That brings to memory the time your daddy was lost out in the desert with your Tios John and Luke."

"Daddy was lost in the desert?" questioned Stephanie, "Here?"

"No, no, not here. The boys know this desert like the back of their hand. No, it was out where Tio Billy had a lease and kept cows in Portal. The boys had gone out to help him fix fence. They'd been dropped off with the materials and instructions to work their way Northwestward while Tio Billy worked Southeastward. They'd meet in the middle having fixed the entire line of fence," she explained.

"So, how were they lost if they were all together?" asked Stephanie.

"That's a very good question, Stephanie," laughed Memaw, thinking back on the story. "I can laugh now, but it wasn't very funny at the time."

"It was coming dark when Tio Billy called Tia Cindy. We'd asked them to call once they were done working and headed home so we could start warming supper. I walked into the kitchen to hear Cindy say, 'Where's the last place you saw them?' Then she said, 'We'll start looking at Stardust Road and work our way up to Geronimo's Pass.' She hung up and told me, 'The boys weren't at the spot they should've met up with Billy at. He went looking for them but they're nowhere to be found.' It turns out Billy had looked for quite some time but knew it was getting dark so thought he'd better get help."

The children lay on their bellies propped up on their elbows looking at Memaw with questioning eyes of concern. Fully enthralled in the tales of when their own daddy was lost in the desert, they were momentarily distracted from worrying about their friend Ben.

"Fear and worry began to creep in to my thoughts and heart. I knew I couldn't give way to fear because fear doesn't come from God.[252] I knew the Enemy would want nothing more than to paralyze me with fear over all that could potentially happen to my boys out there lost in the desert at night. It's not easy to

---

[252] 2 Timothy 1:7

just tell oneself, 'Do not fear!' and it be gone. I had to pray my way there. So that's what we did. We got shoes and jackets on Tia Cindy's kids, put them in their car seats and headed down the highway to go look for the boys."

"You have to know, Tio Billy and Tia Cindy ranch very near the Southern border to Mexico where illegals carrying drugs and guns cross by foot to get their packs sold here in the United States. My worry was more than just my boys being exposed to wild animals and the elements. The illegal activity that happens on full moon nights in that area is a very real and a very dangerous threat," explained Memaw.

"I started glorifying God and thanking Him that the boys were protected by the Blood of Jesus. I proclaimed that we submit to God and resist the devil so he must flee from them[253] and from my thoughts. I prayed that God would put a hedge of protection around them and keep His angels encamped round about them.[254] I prayed and prayed many of God's promises like Psalm 91 that says because we choose to live in the shadow of God Almighty, we are protected by Him and no danger will come near us. I told the devil he was bound from working in the boys' lives—he could not touch them. Because what we bind here on Earth, God binds in and from Heaven.[255] He has given us the authority to do it, we must use it," said Memaw.

Slowly and not realizing it, the children were getting worked up. They sat up and felt armed; instead of lying down, feeling defeated. Still not saying a word, they clung to every word Memaw spoke.

---

[253] James 4:7

[254] Psalm 34:7

[255] Matthew 18:18

She began praying for Ben, "Just like your protection over my boys when they were lost in the desert, Father, we pray for Your protection over Ben and his dog Boots. We ask in the name of Jesus that nothing bad would happen to them. That You would protect them and be present with them wherever they are and that You would direct Ben to the place he should be—whether walking, or to stay put and be found—whatever is safest for him under his present circumstances, Father. Thank You that You love Ben and are taking care of him. Please take care of and comfort his momma and daddy and brother too. May they feel Your comfort and love for them all. Please keep the devil from being able to have his way in that family's life, Lord. May the Enemy's plans be thwarted because no weapon formed against Ben may prosper, in Jesus' name. And we pray that You'd please direct the people who are looking for Ben right to the spot they need to go to find him, Heavenly Father. We pray these things in the mighty, the powerful, and the precious name of Your dear Son, our Lord and Savior, Jesus Christ."

"Amen and amen!" shouted the kids all together. "Thank you for praying for Ben," said Micah. "I feel like he's gonna be okay."

"Obviously your dad and Tios John and Luke were okay, they're alive today," said Olivia. "Tell us how they were found, Memaw?"

"With every mile we drove closer, the sun was setting lower and lower behind the mountain and the land was getting darker and darker. Cindy and I fought the spiritual battle against fear and the devil working in their lives, but not before nightfall. Fortunately, it was a full moon night so the boys had light from above shining down on them as they walked for miles trying to find their way. As I was praying, the Lord showed me that He was leading them just as He had the Israelites with a pillar of fire by night.²⁵⁶ The moon's light being their pillar to light their way. It was most comforting to me to have received that picture from God in that way at that time," she shared.

"So, they didn't have to sleep out in the desert that night?" asked Micah.

"No, fortunately not. Though they walked for hours, they did not sleep out there," sighed Memaw. "No, Billy was smart and parked his pickup on a hill higher than ground level, turned on his headlamps so the boys could see him from wherever they were and hoped they would walk toward the truck lights. That's exactly what they did but it took hours to get there. Meanwhile, Cindy and I were walking the desert, calling out for them from where Billy said they'd started. We could see truck lights in the distance and wondered if they were Billy's and hoped against doubt that they'd be and that the boys had seen them as well and were walking toward the lights."

"Finally, Tio Billy called Tia Cindy and informed us they were back at the pickup with him. We met up so that I could physically see that they were okay and we drove back to their house following the boys."

"What did the boys say?" asked Stephanie. "I bet they were scared."

"Psh, actually," Memaw laughed, "They were exhausted from the miles and miles they had walked but were more embarrassed than anything that they'd gotten lost. You see, they..." Memaw was interrupted by the telephone ringing.

"Ben and Boots are found and home safe," Papa informed.

---

²⁵⁶ Exodus 13:21

"Glory to God Almighty!" exclaimed Memaw. "I'll let the children know. Please tell Ben that Micah will be happy to hear he's home and give the Madrid's our love. See you home soon. Love you," she told Papa.

"Ben and Boots are home safe now, praise the Lord!" announced Memaw.

"Thank You, Jesus." whispered Micah with a sigh of relief.

"Oh Good," said Ezra.

"Thank You, Jesus!" exclaimed Stephanie and Olivia at the same time. They smiled at each other.

"Let's pray," encouraged Memaw, bowing her head. "Heavenly Father, we thank You that You love your children and take care of us. Thank You for helping Ben and Boots to be found and that You protected them and they are home safe. We are so grateful to You."

"Amen," replied the family.

By now, everyone had walked out into the living room to share the news with Momma who'd been praying on the living room sofa after cleaning the kitchen.

Not forgetting Memaw had been in the middle of her story when the phone rang, Ezra asked, "Finish telling us the story of when Dad and his brothers were lost, Memaw."

"Oh, there's not much else to tell after they were found. We all went back to Tio Billy's house and sat down for supper. The boys were worn out. They told the story from their perspective and, wow, it definitely wasn't anything like our perspective. It was more an adventure for them. They were talking about their plans of what they'd do if they had to sleep out there. Of the shelter they planned on building. Of how they planned on digging a hole underneath their shelter to lay in to sleep. Of how they hoped Tio Billy would be grateful they carried the tools and materials back with them and didn't just dump them like they'd wanted to. They were too tired to pack the wire, post driver and t-posts, but didn't want to get in trouble for not," laughed Memaw.

In walked Papa and Daniel just as Micah asked, "How did they say they got lost if they were supposed to fix fence and meet up with Tio Billy half way?"

"They started down the wrong line and were on the neighbor's fence instead of their own." laughed Memaw.

"Mom, are you telling stories on me?" asked Daniel as the entire house erupted with laughter at the thought of the guys fixing the neighbors fence instead of Billy's.

Once the teasing of Daniel simmered down, Memaw continued, "You know, on a serious note, I want you to understand a couple of things. First, the power of prayer. Had we not prayed with authority over the situation, binding the devil from working in our family's lives, the situation could have turned out much differently. If we had not prayed asking God to help protect, be with, and guide the boys out of that trap, they might've had to endure difficult hardship. Prayer must be your first defense in any situation. Through prayer ask for wisdom to know how to handle your present situation and get out safely."

"Daniel, did you and your brothers think to pray that night?" Memaw asked Daniel very seriously.

"We did, but it wasn't yet a formal prayer as if we would've laid in that hole to sleep in. We would have prayed then because we were accustomed to praying when we were in bed; but before that, as we walked along in the desert, it was more like, 'Please God, help us find Billy. I'm so tired'. At one point Luke said, 'Dear God, please don't let us walk up on a snake.' I think acknowledging God for all we need comes naturally when prayer is a part of your normal life," he said.

"That's the way life should be. It blesses my heart you'd thought of going to Him for what you needed," said Memaw.

"Dad, were you afraid?" asked Micah.

"Not yet and not as if I would've been all alone. While we were out there for hours, we were at least together and there was comfort in that. We never got to the point we actually slept out there. Maybe at three in the morning with noises in the bushes and our imaginations going wild it would've been different. So, honestly, no. We were actually kinda excited at the prospect of having to survive out in the desert by ourselves. We thought that would've been cool." answered Daniel.

Memaw rolled her eyes at his answer. "Very cool, Daniel, as Tia Cindy and I were nearly sweating blood over your predicament."

Everyone laughed.

"You know," started Memaw, "there are two sides to every story—in any situation. In an argument, an accident, an account of a story, and in this experience. You don't fully know the perspective of both sides until you hear both sides of the story. They are usually different—sometimes drastically different—one not necessarily right or wrong over the other, but just different one side from the other. But that's a lesson for another day. Right now, we need to get you home since we have church in the morning."

13.

GOD'S PROVISION

*"Beloved, I pray that you may prosper in all things
and be in health, just as your soul prospers."*
3 John 2

There are few activities under the sun as comforting as
front porch sitting. Whether it be starting your morning
there with your Bible surrounded by the cool morning dew and
birds chirping; or you end your day there as the sun sets on the
horizon casting shadows from the trees while you reminisce
on the days' events and tomorrow's plans. Or, like today, with
the overcast sky promising a southeastern Arizona monsoon.
We gathered as Matthew, Michael, Raelene and Reuben were
horseback roping in the front arena.

Papa was coiling and recoiling little Mark's rope after every
throw at the roping dummy. He isn't yet coordinated enough
to gather and recoil his own rope at two, but he looks adorable
throwing it and occasionally getting himself tangled up in it.

All the grandchildren ride horses and some compete in
events, but Matthew is the avid roper who ropes professionally

and is training to compete in the National Finals Rodeo in Nevada. Michael and Raelene are taking turns heading for him.

Around the corner from the side of the house came Briana and Olivia. They'd been sent to take drinks and otter pops to the little ones playing in the fort. They sat in chairs beside Memaw. Briana was in a melancholy mood, though she'd giggle at the teasing and laughing happening in the arena from the ropers and the chute help.

"Looking forward to camp this year?" Memaw asked.

"Yes, ma'am. It won't be the same with so many having aged out, and I was friends with mostly the older kids and cousins, but I am looking forward to it," she smiled.

"What discipline are you getting instruction in?" continued Memaw.

"Barrels and poles again," answered Briana.

"Think you might want to consider Rodeo Bible Camp this year, Olivia?" asked Memaw.

What is it?

A summer youth camp that teaches the Bible, as well as different rodeo disciplines by professional rodeo athletes in their various events. It's a great organization that's centered on teaching God's Word.

"I don't think I'm good enough horseback to do a rodeo event," she answered.

Briana encouraged, "But that's what camp is for, to teach you. Please come, Olivia?"

Olivia responded with a smile.

"Memaw," began Briana with hesitation.

"Yes, Baby?" she answered endearingly caressing Briana's hair while looking her in the eyes.

"I invited my friend, Samantha, to church with us but she said her parents wouldn't allow her to attend because we go to a church that believes in a 'prosperity doctrine'. What does she mean by that? Is that bad? Do we?"

"I see." After thoughtful silence she continued. "I'm glad you're asking and not just carrying this doubt about your church. Did you ask your mom or dad about this?"

"Not yet."

"Okay, well, I guess I could give you my opinion, but you really ought to go to your parents with this one. Will you go to your momma and daddy, even after we talk?" confirmed Memaw.

"Sure."

"Thank you."

"Well, it's my opinion, and that's all it is, just my opinion, that too often people criticize the things which they do not understand. They speak about your church teaching that God does, in fact, desire to prosper His children because perhaps they have not taken the time to search out what the Bible has to say about that topic in particular. The Bible has a lot to say about that, indeed."

Olivia looked up at Memaw for the explanation of this, so called, 'doctrine'.

"Briana, too often, people assume the word 'prosperity' relates only to money and that some churches teach God wants you to be rich with money and how to get it. Yes, in fact, God does teach He wants you to be prosperous but, in mind with wisdom, in body with health and in all that one needs, not just wants, but needs—even financially. '...I pray that in all things you may prosper and be in good health even as your soul prospers.'[257] is how John says it in the Bible."

---

[257] 3 John 1:2

"But, just as with the issue of salvation, God looks at the heart. Salvation isn't sealed just because you say one prayer. Salvation is *believing* Jesus' love for you and learning His Word and walking according to the love it speaks of and teaches. This is what is meant by 'working out your salvation'. Prosperity doesn't happen just because you ask for it once, or because you give money."[258]

Taking a sip of her tea and whispering a prayer for guidance from Holy Spirit, Memaw continued, "First of all, everything belongs to God to begin with.[259] He blesses us with the privilege of taking care of what we have been entrusted with, be it money, a home, a car, or children, or pets—everything."

"Secondly, God asks us to be generous because giving eliminates selfishness and greed from our lives. Learning to give without grieving causes us to learn to rely on God and not ourselves. It's important we develop a generous heart,"[260] she explained further.

"God does not need our money, Briana. He needs our obedience and it's not for His sake, but for our own. If we can obey His Word when we are instructed to give, and do it with a cheerful heart and not a grieving, regretful heart, we open ourselves up to a whole new level of faith. One that glorifies God and is for the good of others, not just our own good."[261]

"I see," was all Briana could say.

"He asks for ten percent of all we earn because that is a fair amount across the board, regardless of how much, or how little one makes. Tithing, or giving ten percent, has been established to support the Church, as that is where we are commanded to

---

[258] Matthew 7:17-23

[259] Psalm 24:1

[260] 2 Corinthians 9:5-12

[261] Matthew 6:21

give our tithe. The Church that feeds us the meat of God's Word; that teaches us how to walk according to God's teaching. The Church that supports us when we go out and minister and witness to others. Without the backing of our churches, we would all be alone and perhaps not as far in knowledge, nor have a place to gather and agree in prayer, which is so important."[262]

"As for churches that teach what people call a 'prosperity doctrine'. Of course, that isn't the only thing they teach, but often people share about or teach what they know, have personally experienced, or have a testimony of, but also, they're just doing their job. How can a pastor know what the Bible teaches and not teach it when it's for the good of the congregation? Some pastors are ridiculed for having a lot of money and it is sometimes assumed that they are extorting money out of their congregation members. But what I wonder is if those people ridiculing have ever studied out God's Word that some of those pastors have studied and are now living testaments of God's principles actually working?"

Memaw looked up into the gray sky with a beam of sunlight coming down to the right of them shining on a rose bush.

She continued, "If people read, learned and followed God's Biblical principles about sowing and reaping would they, too, be walking in health and have their souls prosper as well as their finances? Even God said, '...and test Me in this area...if I will not open for you the windows of heaven and pour out for you such blessing that there will not be room enough to contain it.'[263] Or, do they just categorize those churches and pastors like

---

[262] Malachi 3:10

[263] Malachi 3:10

yours as the teachers of a 'prosperity doctrine' and assume it just doesn't work?'"

"I don't know," answered Briana thoughtfully and not really sure she was getting the answer she needed.

Memaw continued with a surprising statement that made Briana sit up. "Papa and I are one of those that questioned the teaching too."

Looking up at Memaw with surprise and raised eyebrows Olivia, too, got interested.

"Because Papa and I questioned it, we did the research out of the Bible for ourselves. And do you know what we learned?"

"What?"

"We learned that it takes so many hours to research what the Word of God says about giving that we spent not only hours; not only days; not only weeks; but months in His Word learning what He says about His children giving. In doing so, because we were seeking Him and His righteousness, all that we have need of, He makes provision for."[264] said Memaw.

"We learned that the King James Version of the Bible makes mention of some form of the word 'prosperity' over 50 times. And, no, it wasn't speaking against prosperity to make mention of it."

"Over 50 times?" asked Briana surprised.

"Yes," answered Memaw reaching for her cell phone. From the *Notes* section of her phone, she read, "Nineteen times it uses the word *prosper*; 10 times it uses the word *prospered*; 4 times it uses the word *prospereth*; 10 times it uses the word *prosperity*; 7 times it uses the word *prosperous*; and 2 times it uses the word *prosperously*," she read.

"Haha, *prospereth*," giggled Olivia.

---

[264] Matthew 6:33

"Yeah, that is an Old English version of the word. *Prospereth!*" exaggerated Memaw with an English accent.

"That's a lot of discussion about prosperity and that doesn't even include the verses that don't make mention of the specific word, but do refer to the word's same message — and there are many," she added.

"Hmph," was all Briana said, but her outward expression was cheering up.

"That's not all we learned. Want to know more?" Memaw asked.

"Sure!" exclaimed Olivia.

Briana said, "Yeah!"

"We learned that by definition, according to Webster's Dictionary, the word *prosperous* is *to be auspicious, favorable. Marked by success or economic well-being. Enjoying vigorous and healthy growth. Flourishing.*" read Memaw from her *Notes*.

"Do you know that you can be auspicious, favorable and flourishing; growing and healthy in more ways than financially? Especially with God. He wants us flourishing in good health, in wisdom, in power, emotionally and mentally, as well as financially, or He wouldn't have made provision for us to prosper in each those areas. He not only speaks of prospering financially in His Word but, in deed, in wisdom, in health and in power as well.[265] Don't take my word for it, look it up for yourself in the Bible."

Briana smiled at Memaw's enthusiasm over defending the Bible. Though God doesn't need Memaw to defend Him or His Word, Briana was proud of her stance of backing the Word of God all the way.

---

[265] 3 John 2

Without being asked or encouraged, Memaw continued with all she and Papa had learned, "We learned that when you write down each and every reference from the Bible that speaks of God blessing His children's finances; protecting His children's finances; and providing for His children, you do a lot of Bible reading, a lot of Bible study, Bible memorizing and taking Bible notes."

"As a parent myself, I love it when I see my children, or grandchildren," she smiled down at the girls endearingly, "digging into the Word of God and eating it up. What must God feel to see His children completely enthralled in a study of His Word and precepts He's given us for life? Samuel says, 'God honors those that honor Him.' "[266]

"We also learned that God very often prospers those He loves like Solomon and Abraham. David, Joseph, Job and many others. But what stood out to me most is, just like us—your Papa and I aren't perfect—they weren't either, but they followed after God and were committed to Him and His Word and God took care of them."

"He did, didn't He?" agreed Briana.

"We also learned that the Hebrew word BLESSED means 'empowered to prosper and increase'. The Old Testament was written mostly in Hebrew, remember?"

"Yes!" exclaimed Briana.

"And don't we go around telling people we wish God would bless them when we say, 'God bless you'?"

"Yes! Yes, we do!" she laughed.

---

[266] 1 Samuel 2:30

"So, what do you mean when you say those words to someone if not, 'I wish God would empower you to prosper and increase'?"

"I mean for people to be blessed by God." Briana laughed, throwing her hands into the air and leaning back. "I don't know how else to mean it."

"Yes, but while God prospering His children in various forms is Biblical, it must be done God's way; with a cheerful heart, and for the right reasons, like to have more to give more to others.[267] If it's only for personal financial gain, God knows all things.[268] I haven't often seen where God blesses financially when it is for selfish gain only. He desires for us to gain a whole lot more than just money. He wants us to increase in good health and wisdom, too. It's not all about only increasing monetarily to God,"[269] added Memaw.

"And when God does bless you with money, it is so that more money can be used for Kingdom work. The Bible talks about four forms of giving. Tithes, which is 10% of all you earn.[270] Offerings, which is giving above and beyond the tithe.[271] First Fruit offerings are done once a year, at the start of the year.[272] And Alms, which is giving to the poor."[273]

---

[267] Hebrews 13:16

[268] Acts 20:35

[269] 1 Timothy 6:17&18

[270] Malachi 3:10

[271] 2 Corinthians 9:7&8

[272] Deuteronomy 26:2-4

[273] Proverbs 19:17

"Providing for the poor, the widows and the orphans, is our responsibility.[274] We need to take that responsibility seriously. Always ask Holy Spirit what He would have you do with the money you've been given. As well, the Bible talks about giving to the poor in secret.[275] That way we don't get prideful for giving to others. Only God should get the glory for that."

She continued to explain, "The Book of Proverbs explains that a good name,[276] riches, honor, and long life[277] are forms of prosperity too. It also states that, 'He who is generous will be blessed.'[278] There is much said about giving to the poor."[279]

"As well, God says we should rather have a fear of the Lord than great treasure."[280]

"Additionally, and very importantly, we must be tithing and giving offerings. If we are not, we are 'stealing from God'[281] the Bible says in Malachi. Many people believe that tithing being mentioned only in the Old Testament means that we don't have to tithe today because we follow the New Testament. Maybe they are right, but I read in the books of Matthew and Luke when Jesus is correcting the Pharisees telling them, 'you tithe mint and rue and all manner of herbs, and pass by justice and

---

[274] Psalm 82:3

[275] Matthew 6:1-4

[276] Proverbs 22:1

[277] Proverbs 3:16

[278] Proverbs 22:9

[279] Proverbs 28:27

[280] Proverbs 15:16

[281] Malachi 3:8&9

the love of God. These, you ought to have done, without leaving the others undone.' "[282]

"Do you understand that?" asked Memaw.

"I don't." answered Olivia.

"Jesus was telling the Pharisees they tithe, yes, but should offer justice and the love of God, too, without leaving out tithing. So, I do clearly see it in the New Testament, as well."

"There is a lot said about giving in the Bible," decided Briana.

"There is. But God looks at the heart behind the giving and the asking. A heart attitude is of greater importance to Him than a need is, or even the provision for our needs. Too often, our definition of *need* is very different than God's definition of what we *need*.

"God knows we NEED Him and His Word living in us—not just what He and His Word can provide for us. Get the *need* for Him and His Word in us understood, and in the proper order, and there is no limit to what God can do for us!"

"There is a difference, huh!?" agreed Briana.

"Yes, there definitely is. And quite often, the criticizers of the so-called 'prosperity doctrine' tried it and it didn't work for them because their hearts weren't right in the asking; or, they never sought out the Word of God to learn for themselves what He says about His children prospering. Which is a sad fact, in and of itself," added Memaw. "Or, they're not tithing at all."[283]

"I urge you both, Briana and Olivia, like Solomon, desire wisdom from God and all else you need will be added to you—in abundance even.[284] When you choose to follow the wisdom of

---

[282] Luke 11:42

[283] Matthew 23:23

[284] 1 Kings 3:5-14

the Lord, riches don't always equal jewels or silver or gold, but riches do come, and with honor as well. The book of Proverbs says so."[285]

"As well, His Word says that, 'no sorrow comes with God's financial blessing.'[286] Too often, problems come with financial gain from the secular world—not when it is a gift from God."

"Memaw," started Olivia.

"Yes, Sweetheart."

"Why didn't God give me what I needed when I was cold and hungry and didn't have enough to eat?" she asked playing with the straw from her juice drink.

"You're here with us and eating food to your fill; sleeping in a warm bed; and have clothes to wear, don't you? I'd say He provided for you. It isn't always at the time we think we need it, or in the way we feel we need it, but His plans are always better than our plans. We wouldn't have you here with us today if you hadn't gone through all you did, Olivia."

Tears ran down Olivia's face as she leaned in to Memaw's side where she drew comfort and love, every time she needed it. "That's true, huh? He did provide for me."

"Thank You, Jesus," whispered Memaw.

"Thank You, Jesus," said Olivia.

Without a word Briana stood to move around to the other side of Memaw's rocker to hug Olivia.

They sat in silence sipping on their watered-down iced tea. The first few light sprinkles began to come down. Ruben, Raelene and Michael were walking their horses out of the arena and the chute helpers were climbing the panels to exit the arena

---

[285] Proverbs 22:4

[286] Proverbs 10:22

as well. The only one left behind roping the dummy horseback was Matthew. This scene gave Memaw an analogy.

"Girls, who do you see still in the arena?"

"It's Matthew still out there," answered Olivia.

"I guess the others must be hot, tired and thirsty and not wanting to get wet, it looks like here comes the rain," Memaw commented.

"Uh-Huh," agreed Briana.

"Do you think Matthew is hot, tired and thirsty too?" she inquired.

"Probably. But he's training for Finals. He's gonna stay out there — rain or shine, until he can no longer see unless Papa turns on the arena lights for him," added Briana.

"You know your cousin," agreed Memaw. "That's commitment alright."

"He is committed. It's the only way to succeed, Daddy says," repeated Briana.

"And that's why I believe Matthew will do well at the National Finals Rodeo, because he is committed. Will he win first place and take the jackpot? Only God knows and there is no guarantee of it. However, he has already walked out a winner just for getting there. For giving it his best commitment. He will come out a winner in honor, in name, and chances are, financially even if not in first, as succeeding placements get a pretty good chunk of change, too."

To complete her analogy Memaw continued, "Do you know that this is how God wants us to be committed to His Word? Like Matthew is committed to roping. To read it. To study it deeper and deeper. To walk it out. To test it. To teach it to others. To eat, live and breathe it. And just like Matthew at Finals, you will walk victoriously when you learn it and live it out daily.

You can't *not* gain wisdom and thereby prosper in riches and honor and a good name, and yes, even in finances, when you are committed to God and His Word.[287] His Word says so."

Memaw had the girls' complete attention so she went on. "The Word of God says you will reap what you sow.[288] And it is not necessarily talking only about money. It is talking about being kind to people. By sowing gentleness, kindness and patience toward others, you will be treated with gentleness, kindness and patience. Maybe not the same people you sow into, but it will come back to you even if through someone else."

"Sow good works into ministries or people God calls you to sow into, and others will sow into your life's work with things that you need done and help with."

"Sow time into people who need it most and others will give you time in different ways where you need it most."

"Sow your money into the Kingdom of God and in places He directs you to and God will see to it that you have all that you need and, yes, even some desires—just because He can and He is a good God." She paused momentarily.

"Does it ALWAYS work out this way?" asked Briana.

"Not always at the time that we feel we need it most; nor from the people we would like to see it come from. Not always in the manner we would like to see it happen, but yes, the spiritual laws of sowing and reaping do always work—in God's way and in His time."

Memaw continued, "Do pastors or evangelists or ministers ever misuse this spiritual law? Maybe some have misused, even misappropriated the law of sowing and reaping. But I am not

---

[287] Matthew 6:33

[288] Galatians 6:7

here to judge anyone else's actions — that is between them and God and believe the Bible, they will have to answer to God for that if they did," she warned.

"Does the fact that some gave for their own gain and not in the right heart make it altogether wrong?" Without waiting for an answer, "No. Some bad apples give the entire bushel a bad name, but it shouldn't be that way. There are some bankers who don't do what is right all the time, that doesn't make *every* banker a bad banker. There are some used car salesmen who aren't honest, that doesn't make *every* used car salesman a dishonest one. There are some doctors who misdiagnose patients, that doesn't make *every* doctor a bad one altogether."

"The principle remains the same and a working one. The person putting it to work will reap a harvest when it is done according to God's Word — meaning, if it falls under the will of God, is done with the right heart, and asked for after you have forgiven others, and all else the Bible teaches then, yes, it will work. But if it doesn't work exactly as you wanted it to, by the means you intended, or at the time you expected it, it does not mean it doesn't work at all."

"It only means you need to pray and find out what God is trying to tell you."

"Maybe that you shouldn't have whatever it is you're asking for?"

"Maybe that you don't need whatever it is you think you need?"

"Maybe whatever you want is not going to benefit you? He sees all things. He knows all things. We have to trust Him in all things."

"Maybe even, that He has better for you. Or, it just isn't the right time for you to have 'it'. When we trust God with our lives for everything, He does and will take care of us—even when bad things happen."

"Most importantly, we shouldn't give just to get; we should give to bless."

"Papa and I have example, after example, after example of our not getting what we thought we needed at the time we needed it only to find out we, in our human mind with limited knowledge didn't realize what God intended and had for us all along was sooo way better than what we were asking for."

"Trust His will for you. Don't be quick to get angry and be disappointed when you don't get your way, or throw out the possibility that He doesn't bless us with what we ask for, just because it doesn't manifest immediately."

"God is not a genie. We shouldn't treat Him like one. When we trust Him with our lives to do what is right for us and take care of us, we must remember He knows more and better than us. We have to trust He is on it and it will work out for our good. Whenever and whatever does manifest for that particular situation is His will for us and in our best interest—*when* we completely surrender our lives to Him."

"You see, God is interested in helping us grow and fix things, not just to give us all things. He doesn't want to create spoiled rotten brats in us. He is a Good Parent."

"Let me ask you this," asked Memaw, "with as many hours, as much time, attention, prayer and study we've put into the Word of God, are Papa and I rich?"

"No," answered Briana.

"Yes," answered Olivia, simultaneously.

They all laughed to hear entirely opposite answers from entirely different perspectives.

"I would agree we are!" exclaimed Memaw. "Maybe not with money, but we are rich in love, rich in blessings, and have all we need and even some desires that are only wants. However, and most importantly, we have knowledge of God's truths. We have eternal life. We have God's divine hands of safety and protection over our family. And His divine hands of health and healing over us all, too."

She continued after a momentary pause, "We have a Savior to go to for help in times of trouble, and for wisdom in times of questioning. We have authority over Satan's fiery arrows and peace of mind that surpasses our understanding."

"I'd say we are filthy rich!" laughed Memaw out loud.

"All that means we are prospering. And I do believe that, as a good Parent, God wants all His children prospering in every area of life. Not all His children do because it takes *a lot* of time in His Word to learn how to prosper in health and in finances and in wisdom and in peace. But when prosperity doesn't come to us, it's NOT His fault."

Memaw was on a roll..."When it doesn't come out to the advantage of the asker, as they assumed it should, people are too quick to disregard that God answers prayer and go to blaming Him and calling His ways false. When all along, they are actually missing out on growing and learning how to mature spiritually."

"God is Jehovah Jireh, meaning *our Provider*. However, He provides *all* we need, not just monetarily. And, He provides for *every* area of our lives. His work is a complete work that provides much more for us than just *things*."

"I guess I oughta step off this soapbox of mine and get supper warmed up. Everyone is coming in and will be hungry after working so hard. But did I answer your question, Briana?" she asked.

"Yes, ma'am, you did. Thank you, Memaw. I'm glad God is our Provider of all things. We need more than just what we think we need. And prosperity means prospering in a lot more than just money," she restated to show she understood.

"Good job, little one. You are brilliant beyond your years," said Memaw hugging Briana and then Olivia.

Memaw stood from her rocking chair and headed inside to get supper warmed up when she suddenly stopped, turned around and looked at Briana to say, "Sweetheart, one last important thing."

"Yes, Memaw?"

"Believing in this Biblical principle does not make or break your salvation. People don't have to believe it to be saved. They will live in eternity with Jesus even if they don't take advantage of this blessed gift here on earth in the here and now," said Memaw.

"There are some doctrines that are debatable but there are those that are non-negotiable. This one you can let your friend believe whatever they are comfortable believing because every Christian is entitled to believe God's Word for themselves based upon Holy Spirit's leading and guiding and convictions to each individual."

"I would recommend you not correct your friend, as much as encourage her toward the Word of God to study out for herself and ask Holy Spirit for guidance and wisdom. They are saved, and that is what really matters. We cannot judge them for their individual convictions. Understand?" smiled Memaw.

"Yes, ma'am," smiled Briana. "Thank you for helping me understand."

Another hug and Memaw began walking inside when Olivia called out, "Memaw."

"Yes, Mija?"

"Did you know the letter 'z' in the *Cozy Acres Farm* sign hanging from the entryway is backwards?"

Memaw and Briana laughed and laughed before Briana was able to say, "That was my dad that did that."

Through giggles Memaw is able to say, "Yes, Briana's dad made us that sign for Christmas one year."

Briana explained, "My little brother Andrew was playing with the letters and getting them out of order while dad was getting his welding gear on and..." more giggles, "my mom put them all back in place and took Andrew away, but no one noticed the letter 'z' was backwards and dad welded it on that way."

"I love it this way for that reason!" laughed Memaw. "Your Tio Tony wants to take it down to weld it on the right way but I refuse. I love the story and will always think of Andrew as a little tyke 'helping' his daddy make Memaw's and Papa's sign."

Still laughing Memaw, Olivia and Briana walk into the house to find her dad to remind him of what always embarrasses him. Tony hates the sign that way. Memaw loves it— it's settled.

14.

THE RAPTURE
OF THE CHURCH

"For the Lord Himself will descend from Heaven with a shout,
with the voice of an archangel and with the trumpet of God.
And the dead in Christ will rise first. Then we who are
alive and remain shall be caught up together
with them in the clouds to meet the Lord in the air.
And so we shall always be with the Lord."
1 Thessalonians 4:16-17

*P*apa wiped wood glue off his hands to answer the phone. "Good morning Papa, this is Raelene, how are you today?"

"You just made my day better by calling and getting to hear your voice. How are you, Rae?" as the family affectionately calls her.

"I'm good, thanks. Is Memaw available?"

"No, she's picking up groceries with Olivia, but I'll have her call you when you she gets back in."

"Thank you, I really want to sit down with you and Memaw to discuss some hard theological questions," said Raelene.

"Theological ones, huh? We're no theologians, that's for sure," laughed Papa.

"Papa!" laughed Raelene, "Can you and Memaw help me answer a friend's hard questions?"

"I can promise we will meet with you, we'll take any excuse to see you. And we are willing to give you our layman's opinions, but I don't know that we can give you all the right answers theologically. How's that?"

"Good enough for me, Papa James, when can I come over?"

"Darlin', you can come any time you want according to my schedule, I can stop working any time you need. But your Memaw is different, so you'd better talk with her to be sure she can be here when you're thinking of coming by."

"Okay, can you please have her call me when she's back home?" asked Raelene.

"You've got it, Mija. Will that twin of yours be coming, too?

"I doubt it, he's roping tonight and I'm not waiting for him to be available, sorry. Thanks Papa. See you tonight if it works with Memaw. Love you." she hung up excitedly before Papa could return the 'goodbye'.

"Theological questions. Hmph," mumbles Papa to himself with a smile as he goes back to gluing the box he was working on.

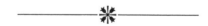

Raelene walked in with blueberries for Memaw and donuts for Papa.

"You were taught well," said Papa reaching for the donuts and handing one to Olivia.

Olivia smiled and said, "Thank you."

"Papa means good manners, not his favorite indulgence, Honey," smiled Memaw as she goes in for a hug and a kiss from her granddaughter. "Thank you for the sweet treats. No pun intended."

"Yeah, thanks, Rae," says Olivia.

"You're welcome," she giggled.

Memaw reaches for the colander to wash the blueberries and asks Olivia for the bowl with the rooster on it. "I understand you have deep questions?" she asks.

"No, theological questions." corrects Papa with index finger up.

"Yes, Memaw, I am so excited. It's my boss at work that's been asking a lot of hard questions. The usual ones that even among Christians themselves get debated," she said.

"Like what?" asked Memaw, popping a blueberry in her mouth.

"Questions like, the age of the earth? What happens when we die? And believing that not being bad or mean or sinning, generally speaking, should secure our salvation. Those I was able to answer, but the more we talk, the more he asks. I honestly think he's going home and reading his Bible or talking to someone. He knows more than he lets off," said Rae. "The questions that really make me think twice, as I said before, are the ones that even Christians debate. How do you explain the Trinity? Will the rapture happen before, during, or after the Tribulation? And, can a Christian lose their salvation?"

"I see. Well, how about we start in prayer. We really need the Lord guiding and directing this conversation and giving us

His wisdom and revelation knowledge of His truths, so let's ask Him for it," encouraged Memaw. She dried her hands and reached for Papa's hand.

Papa James prayed that Holy Spirit would be present giving them wisdom as the book of James tells us, when we need wisdom, all we need do is ask.[289] That He would prick their hearts as they head in wrong directions with their thinking and words, and that He'd keep them lined up with the truths of the Bible. He asked that appropriate Scripture would be brought to their remembrance as they seek answers from the Bible. And that this young man would surrender to God on His own and for his sake. He prayed in the name of Jesus Christ.

"Okay, did you bring your Bible?" asked Memaw. She reached for hers on the counter. Papa walked to the living room for his.

Pulling it out of her bag, "I did," answered Rae.

"Want to follow along, Olivia? Run and grab yours, we'll wait for you," encouraged Memaw.

Olivia ran off and came back with her Bible open.

"Good. Where do we even start?" asks Memaw. "First, I would like to say that those are really good questions. I wonder if he hasn't had some teaching, or influence from a Christian perspective already."

"I have to admit, Raelene, I don't know that Papa and I will have all the right answers. You need to know that we have studied out the scriptures for answers ourselves and have come to different conclusions at different times in our lives. It's all a part of growing in your walk with the Lord," shared Memaw.

---

[289] James 1:5

"I have thought one way about specific doctrines, only to have Holy Spirit convict me when I heard it taught, or read about it in a more thorough teaching that made me change my mind about how I believe particular ones," she admitted. "I believe that is what the Bible means when it says that, 'faith comes from hearing, and hearing from the word of God.'[290]

"And I have to say, initially as a young Christian, it was frustrating to me. I just wanted to know THE right way and attend THE right church that would teach everything accurately right out of the gate. Only to come to the conclusion that there is no perfect church," said Memaw.

Papa added, "Changing your mind about different doctrines should actually happen when you are studying out the Word of God for growth. If you are not learning and changing your thoughts and opinions, you're probably not growing. Because it is rare not to question. It is rare to be taught one way and it be the right way from the beginning about all things."

"Questioning leads to searching the Word of God for answers—that pleases the Lord." said Raelene.

Papa continued, "As a matter of fact, I personally know pastors that have changed their minds about specific teaching and regret that they ever taught a particular topic to have been one way and after further study and prayer and revelation from God, they've changed their minds."

"That is why I have often said, '*I can be easily intrigued, but not easily swayed*'. I have to search out the truths from God's Word and ask Him to reveal to me what I am to believe according to His Word," said Memaw popping blueberries into her mouth.

---

[290] Romans 10:17

191

After swallowing the last bite of his donut and washing it down with milk, Papa added, "The Word of God cautions us not to be easily caught up and taken by every wind of doctrine,[291] however, it's easier done than you realize and before you know it, you're caught up in a whirlwind."

"Ultimately, one must grow and sometimes in growing you get things wrong before you get them right. That is true in business, in school, in ranching, in farming, and just about everything you do—even hunting and fishing."

Raelene and Olivia smiled over what Papa related it to.

He went on, "But those lessons all lead to His Truths. It's not all for naught. The bottom line is—get born again. We need to surrender our lives over to Jesus Christ and receive His forgiveness and grace and choose to make Him Lord over every area of our lives."

Memaw added, "Once that is done, we can continue growing and learning and sometimes making mistakes and failing, but then getting up, asking for forgiveness and striving toward the finish line knowing more, being wiser and getting stronger—not on our own, but with, and in, Christ. Actually, He is to do the work for it to be a complete and accurate work. We can't do the transforming of our own accord. Left on our own, we're a mess!"

"Unless you are saved and have Holy Spirit leading you and guiding you, you **cannot**," Papa emphasized and repeated, "you will not understand the truths of the Bible.[292] Fear of the Lord is the beginning of wisdom.[293] Knowledge can't come

---

[291] Ephesians 4:14

[292] 1 Corinthians 2:14-15

[293] Proverbs 9:10

when you don't have Holy Spirit making the writings of the Bible understandable to you. So be sure you are encouraging your boss, this friend of yours, whomever—everybody you minister to, get born again first and all else will fall into place and eventually make sense for as long as you're asking God and seeking His truths and wisdom from Him and His Word.

"So, what is the first question we can seek the Bible for answers to?" asks Memaw.

"Will the Rapture happen before, during, or after the Tribulation?"

"I'm gonna need another donut for this one," answered Papa reaching for the donut box.

"James," says Memaw as she pretended to be annoyed, rolling her eyes, all the while smiling because he really does make her laugh.

"Well, the Body of Christ is divided on the topic of the timing of the Rapture of the Church. Because the Bible does not distinctly state the time of this inevitable event, as with everything, we pray for wisdom from Holy Spirit and study the Scriptures to learn. It is our opinion that very strong evidence points toward a pre-Tribulation Rapture of the Church," started Papa.

Memaw added, "What was most evident to me in the Scriptures was in Revelation when God tells John, *"Write the things which you have seen, and the things which are, and the things which will take place after this."*[294] The past, present and future tenses He speaks of are then told in chronological order in the book of Revelation. That is so helpful to me as John then covers the **Past** in Chapter 1; the **Present** in Chapters 2 and 3,

---

[294] Revelation 1:19

which is the history of the Seven Churches to the present time; and the **Future** in Chapters 4 - 22."

"In the Book of Revelation, the Church is mentioned sixteen times in Chapters 1-3, but never spoken of in Chapters 6-18 when the Tribulation Period is addressed," Papa explains.

Raelene asked, "Is the Rapture and the Second Coming of Christ one and the same?"

"Very good question, and because there is a difference, this distinction in and of itself is evidence," said Memaw, "At the *Rapture*, Jesus only comes down as far as the clouds and catches us away from there. At the actual *Second Coming*, Christ returns to Earth, specifically to the Mount of Olives, also known as the *Revelation of Christ*."

"Matthew 24:29-31 is a description of the Second Coming, or the Revelation of Christ...the Son of Man comes or appears back on Earth to rule and reign!"

"The Rapture, as spoken of in Revelation chapter 4 is *before* the Tribulation and is a catching away in the air, wherein the Believers are removed from the Tribulation spoken of in chapters 6-18. The Revelation of Christ or His 'Second Coming', spoken of in chapter 19, is *after* the Tribulation, wherein Jesus Christ returns to earth riding a white horse with the Believers following Him. Make sense?" asked Memaw.

"I did look up the word RAPTURE, and by definition, it means "to be caught up or taken away," shared Rae.

"Yes, and a verse in Thessalonians talks about those who are 'alive' being 'caught up' to meet the Lord 'in the air.' *'For the Lord Himself will descend from heaven with a shout, with the voice of an archangel, and with the trumpet of God. And the dead in Christ will rise first. Then we who are alive and remain,'* on earth and still alive" added Memaw for emphasis, " '*shall be caught up together with them in the clouds to meet the Lord in the air. And thus, we shall always be with the Lord.*' "[295]

Memaw was reading the Bible so Papa takes advantage of her being distracted and goes in for a third donut. His hand touches the box when mid-sentence, and without looking up, Memaw gently pushes his hand away without skipping a beat.

Olivia laughs at Papa's antics and Memaw's knowing.

Memaw continues reading unphased.

Papa sat looking like the proverbial child who got caught with his hand in the cookie jar.

Looking up after finishing the text Memaw adds, "That was in First Thessalonians, in Second Thessalonians chapter 2, verses 6 through 8 it says, '*And now you know what is restraining, that he may be revealed in his own time. For the mystery of lawlessness is already at work; only He who now restrains will do so until He is taken out of the way. And then the lawless one will be revealed, whom the Lord will consume with the breath of His mouth and destroy with the brightness of His coming.*' "

"The 'lawless one' refers to the Anti-Christ because in the very next verse it says Jesus will destroy him when Jesus comes back at His Second Coming. As well, the "H" in the word "He" in verse 7 is uppercased in the New King James Version; this means "He" is referring to either God, Jesus, or Holy Spirit. Some say Holy Spirit is the restrainer. Some say that since it is Holy Spirit that lives inside all Believers here in this world it is Holy Spirit in us that make us, His Church, the *restrainers*.

---

[295] 1 Thessalonians 4:16 & 17

Thereby until we, the restrainers, are taken out of the way can the lawless one begin his work," she concluded.

Papa, getting back in the game adds, "If the Body of Christ were still here during the Anti-Christ's introduction, he would not be able to fully rise to the extent of evil with the power Satan is giving him as the Bible describes. Through the powerful TV ministries, radio ministries, and social media sharing, the true Believers would recognize him and spread the word of his identity and pray against his power taking affect—can you see the Church not praying against his work?"

"Of course not," answers Raelene.

"Once we, the Church, are gone there will be nothing left that will be able to restrain the Anti-Christ from rising to full power as the Bible describes will happen."

"So true," said Raelene, "It all makes so much sense."

"A teaching given by Perry Stone, a Pastor, condensed it into a very easy-to-understand manner when he told it from a Hebraic perspective. He said that at the time of Passover, barley is harvested around March or April."

"At the time of Pentecost, wheat is harvested around May or June."

"At the time of Tabernacles, fruit is harvested (olives, grapes, etc.) around August or September."

"In a harvest field, the first fruits are gathered first—before you got everything from the field you went at Passover and got the First Fruits and *separated them out* and took them *to the Temple first*. Leviticus 23:10 "Speak to the children of Israel, and say to them, 'When you come into the land which I give to you, and reap its harvest, then you shall bring a sheaf of the first fruits of your harvest to the priest.'..."

"Once the first fruits are taken the other field is allowed to ripen. Then you get the main harvest. When you reap the main harvest of your land, you do not reap the four corners of the field. Leviticus 19:9 "When you reap the harvest of your land, you shall not wholly reap the corners of your field, nor shall you gather the gleanings of your harvest.""

Flipping to the New Testament Memaw read, "Matthew 24:31 speaks of the gleaning of the four corners, which is the last part of the harvest. 'And He will send His angels with a great sound of a trumpet, and they will gather together His elect' (the 144,000 Jews) 'from the four winds, from one end of heaven to the other.' ""

"At the barley harvest during Passover, when the First Fruits are separated out and taken to the Temple first, there is no use of leaven for seven days, leaven is a representation of sin; when you get to Pentecost leaven *is* used — during the Tribulation, those going through the Tribulation will be dealing with sin (leaven) on the earth but the Church happens to be separated out from that before the start of it — they are the overcomers who are initially raptured," recounted Memaw.

"Fascinating," whispered Raelene, overcome at God's amazing plans and how He is so precise.

"Wait! There's more!" exclaimed Papa, with his index finger in the air. "Because history tends to repeat itself, but mostly because God is a merciful God, think about when He destroyed Sodom and Gomorrah. He allowed Lot to depart before the destruction.[296] Also, Noah and his family were allowed to embark on the ark and evade death by the flood that would

---

[296] Genesis 19:29

197

destroy everything on the earth.[297] The Hebrews were allowed to escape the Destroying Angel.[298] This, I believe, is a picture of God's grace toward His children. Throughout the Old Testament, He had time and time again, warned the Israelites that if they would just repent and turn from their ways, He would forgive them."[299]

As if Rae hadn't been star-struck before over God's awesomeness, she is floored that His ways continue to be revealed. "God is so amazing and so merciful," she says with awe.

"I will end with the clincher," says Memaw. "There is a parallel comparison of the ancient Jewish wedding to the Marriage Supper of the Lamb. Just as in ancient Jewish times, the groom would leave his father's house and travel to his prospective bride's home. Jesus will leave His home in Heaven and come here to obtain His bride, the Church."[300]

"Wow," is all Rae could say.

"Just as the Jewish parents of the groom would pay a price for the bride to her family, Jesus paid a price, with the shedding of His blood, for His bride, the Church, as well,"[301] smiled Papa.

Memaw adds, "Yes, and after the Jewish bridegroom married his bride, he would leave her at her parents' home and go back to his father's house to prepare a home of their own that he would eventually bring his bride to. Jesus, too..."

Raelene cuts Memaw off to finish her statement, "... returned to His Father's home after His resurrection and is

---

[297] Genesis 7:16 & 23

[298] Exodus 12:22-23

[299] 2 Chronicles 7:14

[300] 1 Thessalonians 4:16&17

[301] 1 Corinthians 6:20

now preparing a home for each of us until His return to catch us away to take us back with Him!"[302]

"That's right," answers Memaw with a giggle over Rae's excitement of God's revealed truths.

Then Memaw continues, "When the home was complete and ready, the Jewish bridegroom would show up on an unannounced night to suddenly take his bride. Jesus will one day come in the clouds unannounced and suddenly take us, His Bride, away too."[303]

"So cool!" says wide-eyed Raelene.

Smiling, Memaw continues, "As the bridegroom made the trek, together with his accompanying 'groomsmen' to her home, the townspeople seeing the bridegroom coming would shout, 'Behold, the bridegroom comes!' in order to warn the bride to be ready for here he comes! Jesus, too, will come with an 'escort' the Bible says, 'an archangel'. And His announcement will be by the sound of a loud trumpet."[304]

Papa concluded, "The bridegroom and his 'groomsmen' would not go in all the way, but would stop outside her home and the bride would come out to meet him. After she came out of her home with her matrons of honor they would all, in a procession, go back to the bridegroom's father's house, where her new home was built, for them to consummate their marriage in a bridal chamber called the chuppah, wherein they would hide away by themselves for seven days. At the end of seven days the groom would come out of the bridal chamber and reveal who his bride is. Likewise, the bridegroom, Jesus, will

---

[302] John 14:3

[303] Revelation 16:15

[304] 1 Thessalonians 4:16

go in hiding with His bride, the Church, for seven years, not days, and after the seven years, we will all come out of Heaven and return back to earth to live out the Thousand Year Reign with Jesus." [305]

"So you see? This is why we believe in the pre-Tribulation Rapture of the Church."

"I do see. And it is all eye-opening that all along in His Word, God is showing us future things," said Raelene.

"Yes, however, people interpret His Word differently. Who is right and who is wrong? I don't know. And frankly, wouldn't be surprised if it is slightly different from everyone's points of view. We don't know all things, only He does," [306] smiled Memaw.

"I am excited and overwhelmed by all this that I want to go home and write it all down. I'll have to ask the other questions at another time. Thank you so much for your time and help." said Raelene, quickly packing up her Bible in her bag and reaching for her purse and keys.

She kissed and hugged Memaw, Olivia and Papa and ran out the door.

"Where do I read about this in my Bible, Papa?" asked Olivia.

"I will write down all the places in the Bible this is spoken of for you, and basically, read the entire Book of Revelation," answered Papa.

"Thank you," she said with a smile.

"You're welcome. Ask questions if you don't understand something," he added.

"I will," she left the kitchen toward her bedroom.

---

[305] Revelation 19:8&14

[306] Psalm 147:5

"They're so adorable," said Memaw to Papa.

"I love to see them learning the Word of God," he answered.

"Me too," she said, clearing the sink to wash up the few dishes left on the counter.

Olivia, turning back to stand at the doorway of the kitchen said, "Memaw?"

"Yes, Sweet Girl?"

"I'm ready to be sure I've surrendered my life to Jesus and that He would do the transforming work in me. Would you and Papa pray with me?"

"It would be our honor to," she said with tears filling her eyes. Then turning to Papa, she said, "We have a special birthday cake to make. Today is Olivia's spiritual birthday," she smiled.

Papa wiped away a stray tear, not able to say a word.

Acknowledgements

A heartfelt note of gratitude I extend to my Heavenly Father for Your unending love and guidance. This vision to write children's books You gave me in 1996 and after twenty-six years, here it is. Please continue to teach me to love others as You do and be my Guide. Thank You, Father. I love You!

To my hard-working husband, Jaime, who is always supportive of my turning on the light in the middle of the night to write the thought or word given me by my Guide. I love you and appreciate you for the wonderful husband, father, and now, Papa, that you are! Here's to many more years of growing old together to offer turquoise nuggets to our grandchildren and great-grandchildren and many others we continue to 'adopt' together. Thank you for walking this path with me.

To my seven children whom, without my experiences of raising you, I couldn't be the Memaw that I am to give out any *nuggets* to your children. Thank you for loving me—even when I messed up. Thank you for forgiving me when I was wrong. Thank you for understanding me when I changed my mind. Thank you for supporting me when I was weak. Thank you for allowing me to share some of your life's experiences with others. And thank you for giving me grandchildren. I love you all!

To my momma, who is a special and fantastic Grandma to my children. Thank you, Momma, I love you.

To Stacy Panneck, for the prophetic word that helped inspire me to follow through with this calling on my life and for the friend, supporter and prayer partner that you are. I appreciate and love you.

To Jeff Panneck, with much gratitude I thank you for your assistance in proofreading my manuscript.

To Chris Fabry, my friend, mentor and teacher. I couldn't have done this without your assistance, correction and encouragement. I appreciate you tremendously.

Note from the Author

Thank you to all the Christian families who offer a safe, healthy, loving environment for children from the foster care system to grow up in and be surrounded by love, acceptance, and a chance at life raised in the love and admonition of the Lord. You are a testament to the fact that not all foster care systems, foster homes and foster parents are bad situations. God bless you for your service!

Note to All Children

*A*s Olivia learned, I hope you learn that the goal isn't only about saying one single prayer to get to Heaven and you stop there. It's about getting Heaven into you here and now, on this earth, today. You are very much loved by a merciful Savior, we want you to know how much and why — because He created you, in His image, to shine before men. That changes everything! When you realize that, get alone and think about the Ten Commandments from Exodus 20:3-17.

1 – You shall have no other gods before Me (love only the one true God).

2 – You shall not make idols of anything (your cell phones, tv, people).

3 – You shall not take the name of the Lord your God in vain (honor His holy name and don't trash it).

4 – Remember the Sabbath day, to keep it holy (read your Bible and pray and talk to Jesus).

5 – Honor your mother and your father (love and respect them).

6 – You shall not murder (hating your brother is murder too).

7 – You shall not commit adultery (lusting over another is the same as adultery).

8 – You shall not steal (if it's not yours, don't take it).

9 – You shall not bear false witness against your neighbor (don't lie or gossip).

10 –You shall not covet (want what other people have).

Have you ever broken any one of these? I was devastated when I asked myself this question. I had, and not only one of these, but ALL of them. When I read the first one and realized I had broken it I was crushed. To then have continued down the list and admitted I had broken them ALL, I was devastated. I realized then I need Jesus as my Savior. I can't do life without Him. I don't want to do life without Him.

Ask yourself if you've broken any one of His Commandments. Then tell God how sorry you are that you have sinned and that you don't want to be sinning, but you need Him to help you. Sincerely ask God to forgive you and be so sorry for your sin that you don't want to continue in sin. Tell Him you are willing to let Holy Spirit come in and change you into being His child.

If ever the devil tries to convince you that everybody breaks these all the time, it's impossible not to break them. Offer yourself to God first, then tell the devil, *"NO! You may not work in my life in Jesus' name! I am a child of the Most High God and you cannot touch me! I submit to God and command you to go away from me in Jesus' name!"* He will leave you if you submit to God first.

Just like having a relationship with any other person, you learn who they are, to then become close friends. You want Jesus to be your best friend. These are difficult times we live in with evil all around us. Times of uncertainty with battles over politics and laws and the best way for everyone to stay healthy. We must go to Jesus for wisdom, guidance and direction when it comes to making friends, making choices and not only knowing right from wrong, but choosing to do right over wrong.

You can go to Jesus for protection and for help in times of trouble and to battle feelings that are not healthy about ourselves and about others so we don't wallow in feeling sorry for ourselves, or easily get angry with others.

Jesus also wants to hear from us when all things are going really well and we're doing great. We thank Him and praise Him for His mercies and for showering us with love.

He wants to be a part of our everyday lives—the good and the bad. Learn to include Him and you learn to hear His voice as He directs and guides you. *Pray without stopping*, the Bible says. That means talk to Him all day long.

Bad things and tough situations will still happen because we live in a sinful world. Having Jesus as Savior won't stop that. But when we are seeking the Lord, we are comforted and rest with confidence that He knows what we are going through. He is holding us in His strong hand. He catches and stores our tears when we cry and He rejoices when we are happy. And we quickly learn how to turn bad experiences into good lessons and bad things that happen into examples of how to help other people through similar situations so they don't have to battle alone. We learn that it is better to be bold in doing Christ's work than it is to do work that produces evil.

I encourage you to raise your hands to worship the Lord and tell Him, "My God is so big, so strong and so mighty, there's nothing my God cannot do! You are awesome, God, and I love you!"

Tell others they can be forgiven of their sins if they go to God with a sincere heart and repent of any Commandments they have broken and get reborn into a new creature in Christ.

I rejoice with you and welcome you to God's family. The next step is to ask the grown-up in charge of you, if you could start attending a good Bible-teaching church. But most importantly, and above all, read the Bible. Talk to Jesus. Ask Him questions and learn to hear Him. He will speak to you through His Word and through peace given from Holy Spirit, as well as through other people.

God bless you, friend. I love you, but God loves you even more.